No More No Name

Tim Tingle

7th Generation
Summertown, Tennessee

Library of Congress Cataloging-in-Publication Data

Names: Tingle, Tim, author.
Title: No more No Name / Tim Tingle.
Description: Summertown, Tennessee : 7th Generation, [2017] |
    Sequel to: No Name. | Summary: Life is better for Choctaw teenager
    Bobby Byington as he returns to the basketball team, helps teammate
    Lloyd and neighbor Faye through some difficulties, and sees his
    family drawing close again.
Identifiers: LCCN 2017017315 | ISBN 9781939053176 (pbk.)
Subjects: | CYAC: Basketball—Fiction. | Friendship—Fiction. | Choctaw
    Indians—Fiction. | Indians of North America—Oklahoma—Fiction. |
    Family life—Oklahoma—Fiction. | Fathers and sons—Fiction. |
    Bullying—Fiction. | Oklahoma—Fiction.
Classification: LCC PZ7.T489 Nn 2017 | DDC [Fic]—dc23
LC record available at https://lccn.loc.gov/2017017315

© 2017 Tim Tingle

Cover design: John Wincek

MIX
Paper from
responsible sources
FSC www.fsc.org **FSC® C005010**

7th Generation
an imprint of Book Publishing Company
PO Box 99, Summertown, TN 38483
888-260-8458
bookpubco.com
nativevoicesbooks.com

ISBN: 978-1-939053-17-6

22 21 20 19 18 17   1 2 3 4 5 6 7 8 9

Contents

Contents

CHAPTER 1

Road to Recovery

"Sure you'll be hoke?" Dad asked. He and Mom, for the first time I can remember, were going grocery shopping together.

Now that Dad had stopped drinking, everything changed. Well, not everything. At least not right away. Dad was still nervous and fidgety, and I knew it was not easy for him—staying away from the bottle.

"You sure you're hoke by yourself?" Dad asked.

"Thanks for asking, Dad. I'll be fine. Take your time and bring something good home for supper," I said, spinning my new leather basketball on the fingers of my left hand.

Yeah, it's a little show-offy, but I'd rather Mom and Dad laugh when they think of me, instead of worry.

A month has passed since I drove my friend's car through a metal fence and into Lake Thunderbird, almost drowning.

As I lay in my hospital bed, with burning lungs and unable to talk, I had thought of "No Name," the old Choctaw story. Coach Robison, himself a Choctaw, had told me the story to give me hope in dealing with my dad.

The boy in the story is a good kid, but he doesn't excel at anything. So he hasn't earned a name. And his father is so ashamed of him, shouting and shoving and making the boy— No Name they call him—want to crawl into a hole.

In so many ways I was like the boy in the story. As I struggled to survive, I realized I wanted, more than anything, for my father to respect me. He treated me like I didn't exist. Like the boy in the story, I hadn't earned a name by being good at something, especially something Dad would respect.

I promised myself that if I got through this alive, I'd tell him, "No more No Name, Dad. I am your son, Bobby, and I deserve to be heard."

And now? I am making a name for myself on the basketball court. No more No Name for me! And since I *am* alive, I have to convince the adults in my life that I can still play basketball.

So that's my goal. Happy parents, together again, and happy me—firing away three-pointers. And happy Coach Robison if some of my shots actually hit the bottom of the net.

After a few weeks stuck at home, I am on the "road to recovery," as it's called. From walking to jogging to slapping the backboard, I am now allowed to dribble and shoot free throws and set shots.

"But no jumpers and no scrimmaging. That's doctor's orders," said Coach Robison on my first day of basketball practice.

"I understand," I said. I couldn't wait to be on the court again.

"Bobby?" he asked, with a tilt of his head.

"Yes, Coach?"

"I am as excited as you are to have you back. We lost three games we could have won while you were gone. But no risks! We want this to work. Understand?"

"Yes, Coach Robison, I promise. No risks."

I didn't want to make a big deal out of it, so I waited till my teammates were dressed and on the court. When I heard the pound of a ball on the court and the ughs and tugs of under-the-basket battles, I stepped from the dressing room.

I looked to the floor and carried the ball under my left arm, casual and quiet. Did not work. As soon as Johnny saw me, he shouted, "Yo! Give it up for Bobby Byington!"

This had to be preplanned.

The whole team turned my way and started stomping the floor and cheering in unison: "Bob-EEE, Bob-EEE, Bob-EEE!"

Hoke, I gotta do something. I took three easy dribbles and launched a twenty-foot set shot from the corner. In a dream world, it would have hit nothing but net, and the cheers would be heard all the way to the NCAA finals. Wherever that might be.

But this is no dream world. I missed everything. Air ball.

The cheering stopped. But we Indians stick together. My buddy Johnny—my Cherokee buddy Johnny—snatched the ball as it flew under the goal and laid it in the basket.

"Nice dime," he shouted. "Now, your turn—on my dime."

He tossed me the ball.

I caught it in stride, then took three quick dribbles till I stood at the head of the three-point line. I took one more dribble, stepping back to maybe twenty-seven feet from the basket, and took a high, arching shot.

Total silence.

Till the basketball split the cords.

Bobby was back.

Cheers and backslaps and handshakes from everyone, and I said a little prayer of thanks to whatever Choctaw ancestor guided my shot to the basket. Choctaw habits never go away.

Finally Coach Robison blew his whistle and walked to center court. "Quite a welcome home, huh, Bobby?"

"Thank you, guys," I said. "Glad to be back."

"Now, let's get back to work, boys. Bobby, you can watch or shoot at a side basket. Just remember what we talked about."

I nodded and dribbled to the end of the gym to shoot free throws. When practice was over, Johnny joined me, and we shot our usual ten free throws. He made seven, and I hit all ten.

"Aww, man," he said. "I been working all year on my shot from the line. So you've been on your back for a month, and you still beat me?"

"Some got it, some don't," I said.

"Oh yeah? Let's do double or nothing for a dollar. All you gotta do is make one more. You make it, you win. You miss, I get the dollar."

"I'm guessing you've got enough gas money to get home, 'cause I'm taking your greenback," I said.

I stepped to the line, and Johnny lined up as if to rebound. *As if.* I took my usual two dribbles, then shot the ball to the basket, holding my follow-through and pointing to the sky.

As if. Johnny two-stepped into a crouch before rising a foot above the rim with his fist knotted. He slammed the basketball across the gym and into the bleachers.

"Keep your dollar, young man," he said, strutting to the dressing room. "Use it to buy a slice of humble pie on your way home."

"Welcome back, Bobby," Coach Robison said as I passed by the open door to his office. "Just so you know, I think Johnny missed you more than anyone. You saw the last game, didn't you?"

"Yes, and I thought we were gonna come back and win it."

"You saw how rough it was for Johnny to get the ball under the basket. They double-teamed him the whole game."

"What can I do about that, Coach? I'm a guard."

"Yes, and when you are hitting the long shots, they can't double-team Johnny."

I nodded and smiled. This was a good day. Achukma.

CHAPTER 2

Bully Girl Heather

When I left the gym, Mystery Lady Faye was waiting on the sidewalk. My newly arrived next-door neighbor from North Carolina, Faye was more than a friend.

"Are you waiting for me?" I asked.

"Yes. I just wanted to see you," she said, turning away so I couldn't see her face.

Uh-oh. This always means trouble. Well, not always. She has this crazy way of flirting, and sometimes I can't tell *romance* from *problem*.

"You're worried about my first day of basketball practice and wanted to check up on me, right?" I knew it was a lie.

"Sure, Bobby. You know what a big fan of sports I am. Isn't basketball where you kick it through the goal?"

We walked a few minutes without saying a word. A cloud hung over us, and I had no idea why.

Finally, as we passed a park bench, she spoke. "Do you know Heather?" she asked.

"Sure, she's been in my grade since elementary school. We both used to give teachers a hard time, till they started putting us in separate classes."

"Well, she's not picking on the teachers anymore."

I stopped and looked at Faye, and this time she lifted her face and let me see the pain she was feeling.

I took her hand and led her to the bench, in the shade of a maple tree. "Why is she giving you a hard time?" I asked.

"She gets mad when I make good grades."

"Yeah, that never happened to her," I added sarcastically.

"No, and she won't leave it alone. I'm a 'silly little Southern girl who likes books more than boys.' She says it every time she sees me in the hall. She flips her hair and prances, mocking me up and down the hall."

"And her friends surround her, laughing and pointing at you."

"Sounds like you've been there before," she said.

"Oh yes, me and Johnny both. You maybe noticed there aren't that many Indians in high school here."

"How did you stop the teasing?"

"This might sound crazy, but Johnny and I took the same road to respect."

"What road is that? Can I join you?" she said. Her voice sounded like she was about to cry.

Please. I do not want to comfort Mystery Lady Faye in a public park. Please.

"Sure, you can join us, but it might be too late."

"Too late to protect me. How can you say that?" Now she did start crying, quietly and hoping I wouldn't notice.

"Hey, Faye. I'm your friend, and I'll help you any way I can. You know that. You're always there for me when I need you." I wrapped my arm around her shoulder.

"Thank you, Bobby. I needed that. But why . . ."

"Faye, Johnny and I play basketball. We are both starters on the team, and we've worked hard since we were little kids to get where we are. Even the biggest school bullies can't pick on athletes. The other players, the Nahullos, the white guys, won't allow it."

"So sports—football, basketball, baseball, volleyball, track and field—that's the answer to racism? Oh, I almost forgot swimming."

That's Faye for you. Digging deeper and asking the kind of questions that earn those A's in every class she takes.

"No," I said, "it's not that way everywhere, but that's how things work here."

"Are you telling me that if you weren't a star on the basketball team, you would be pushed around and bullied in the hallways?"

I leaned forward and dribbled a few times on the grass, till the ball hit a stone and rolled a few feet away.

"Yes," I whispered, and for the first time in my life, I realized what Johnny and I had accepted. We snuck through the door because we are ballplayers. Something is wrong with that, way wrong.

We sat on the bench for a long while without speaking.

"Things were better when I was invisible and nobody knew me," Faye said. "It all started in English class when Mrs. Lee talked to me before class about my favorite books."

"I'm guessing you didn't tell her *The Cat in the Hat*."

"No, Bobby, but I wish I had. Maybe she wouldn't have embarrassed me by bragging in class about 'the new girl who loves to read.'"

"She said that? Man, talk about a target. 'The new girl who loves to read.' Yeah, I can hear Heather making fun of that."

"I have to admit, she's good at it. She walked behind me in the library yesterday, and I thought she might leave me alone, but she couldn't do it. She leaned over the table and talked loud enough for all her friends to hear."

"What did she say?" I asked.

"She didn't *say* it, Bobby. She *screamed* it. 'We know you love your books, but the rules say "No making out in the library!"' I wanted to vanish."

"No way!"

"Yes, Bobby. And I know what you're thinking. It's kinda funny unless you're the one she's making fun of."

"What I'm thinking is how to make your life less miserable, Faye. You're my, uh, best friend. You know?"

She took my hand and said in her sweetest Southern voice, "I care for you almost as much as I love John Steinbeck, Bobby."

"John who?"

"Never mind."

"Hey, I'm kidding! I know who John Steinbeck is."

"So, any ideas about how to make my life less miserable?"

"Not gonna be easy," I said. "Wouldn't work for a Choctaw boy to say something to a pretty young Nahullo."

"Bobby, it helps just having you on my side. At least somebody cares."

We were making jokes now, but I had a sudden thought. *Faye was crying just a minute ago.* "You're not telling me everything, are you?" I asked.

Faye closed her eyes and lowered her head to her chest. "No," she said. "I don't want to make you mad."

"What did she do? Tell me. I promise I won't do anything foolish, but I've got to know."

"When I ignored her in the library, she pulled my hair and jerked my head around. Even her friends stopped laughing and moved away."

I stood up and felt my heart pounding in my chest.

"You promised, Bobby. No trouble. She's not worth it."

What happened next flowed like a river in heavy rainfall, unstoppable and fierce. I wrapped my arms around her and pulled her close, then I kissed her with a feeling I had never known before.

CHAPTER 3

Basketball, Yes!

"I've got to go," I said, as I stood up and backed away from the bench. Faye was still in shock.

"Hey, I meant that," I said. "That . . . you know. I just have to be alone."

"I know where you're going. Is it because of me?"

I took a deep breath and did my best to relax. "Yes and no," I said. "It is because I care for you and want to think this thing through."

"Do you want me to join you later?"

"No, Faye. Please understand. I just need some alone time."

"I could use some myself, Bobby." As I turned to go she cleared her throat, in that loud and funny way that means "I have something else to say."

"What?" I asked, turning back to her.

"I was going to say 'Oh, Bobby, please don't forget me,' but I decided not to."

"No you weren't," I said. "You're not that dumb." Before she could reply, I took off running. And I ran hard and I ran fast, through the field in back of our neighborhood. I had to take it easy in front of Coach Robison, but I also had to get in shape. When he called my name, I wanted to be ready. I had a lot to prove.

As Faye had guessed, I dashed to my backyard, to the underground hideaway I had dug last summer—to get away from my dad. I pulled the door aside and leapt into my hidden home, sliding the door over my head.

"Did you miss me?" I asked.

It had been several weeks since I'd been here. I almost expected a deep voice to reply, "Welcome home, Bobby Byington."

But no, only silence. Sweet, blessed silence. At last. I wrapped myself in my old Choctaw blanket and let sleep have its way. I dreamed of the night that changed everything.

My first basketball game as a varsity starter. For the first few minutes, I shiver—feeling out of place and uncomfortable. Then I have the ball in my hands and my confidence soars. One shot drops through the net, and the crowd roars.

I've never heard anybody cheer when I make a shot! I like this. The next shot also hits nothing but net, and by halftime I've scored fifteen points to lead my team. No more No Name!

"Bobby! Are you down there?" My eyes popped open, and the cheering crowd disappeared.

"Yes, I'm here. Is that you, Johnny? Why all the pounding?"

Johnny flung back the door and jumped into my room.

"Your mom and dad came to the gym looking for you. I told 'em you left half an hour ago."

"Is anything wrong?"

"No, I think they just wanted to see how you did at basketball practice. They're probably worrying about you. Get your hiney to supper, you Choctaw caveman."

"Yeah, hoke, Cherokee flagpole, I'm on my way," I said, as Johnny lifted me up and I rolled to the ground above. Through the window I saw Mom setting the table and Dad sipping his evening coffee.

"Thanks, Johnny," I said. "See you tomorrow."

"If you're lucky!" he shouted over his shoulder.

Supper was as good as it gets: pan-grilled pork chops, corn on the cob, and mashed potatoes and gravy. And I didn't ask, but I saw something hidden under a covered dish on the stove. Dessert, no doubt.

"Your mom knows how to make a man happy," Dad said, wiping his plate clean with a hot buttered biscuit.

"Bobby, will you get the ice cream from the freezer?" Mom said. She lifted the cover and placed a bubbly-hot cherry pie in the center of the table.

"Hoke, Mom, is this taking the place of Christmas, or what is going on?" I asked.

"Bobby, your dad and I want you to know how happy we are to be together."

"For the first time, truly together," said Dad, smiling and nodding his head at Mom.

I was slicing my spoon through a scoop of vanilla ice cream sitting atop the cherry pie, when the doorbell sounded. We all looked at each other, and then looked at the wall clock, thinking the same thing. *It's a little late for a visitor.*

"I'll get it," I said, hopping up and dashing to the door. "Coach Robison, what brings you here?"

"Bobby," Dad said, "show some respect."

"Uh, sorry, Coach. I mean, come right in. Would you like some coffee?"

"That's better, son," Dad said, then turned to his old friend and my coach. "Coach Robison, what brings you here?" he asked.

"Dad!"

Everybody laughed as Coach took a seat on the sofa and I brought him a hot cup of coffee. Mom soon appeared, carrying a saucer of cherry pie with melting ice cream on top.

"I should come over more often," he said, spreading his arms and smiling. We waited for his answer to the question hanging in the air. Dad laughed quietly as Coach Robison enjoyed a spoonful of Mom's best dessert ever. He took a long sip of coffee, wiped his face with his napkin, and sat up straight.

"Guess I'd better tell you why I came. Hoke, my plan was to let Bobby know he could begin practicing with the team . . ."

Then he paused. My heart pounded loud enough for the whole neighborhood to hear.

"When?" I asked.

"I was thinking after Christmas."

"Coach, that's a month away! I want to play now! I am in shape and healthy, and I don't want to wait another day."

Mom looked at Dad. Dad looked at Mom. They decided to let Coach Robison take charge.

"Now, wait a minute, Bobby," Coach said. "You need to listen. I clearly said it was my plan that you practice with the team after Christmas. It *was* my plan. But after talking to the team about it, my plan has changed. We want you to join the team for full workouts starting tomorrow."

"Yes!" I shouted, leaping high and slapping the ceiling fan. It was turned off, but the wooden fan blades seemed to echo my cheers, spinning and dancing above us.

"Unless you lose a few fingers celebrating," Coach said, "in which case we might have to wait till Friday."

Mom was clapping and Dad laughed out loud.

"You're a good man, Robison," Dad said, fist-bumping Coach's shoulder. "A good man."

The grown-up fun talk and celebrating continued till Coach Robison finished his pie and coffee. "Time for me to get home," he said. "Bobby, get a good night's sleep. I hope you're in as good a shape as Johnny says, or you'll have a tough day tomorrow."

As he eased his car out of the driveway, I saw Johnny standing across the street. I stepped outside and waved to him.

"Thank you, Johnny. Yakoke," I said.

"Dime back atcha," he answered.

I was glad to share the moment with Johnny. But the one person I wanted to tell more than anybody in the world was next door—crying herself to sleep.

"I'll make it right, Faye," I whispered. "I don't know how, but I'll make it right."

CHAPTER 4

The Kicking Tree

I had never walked anybody to school before. I had already decided I wasn't going to wait for her on the sidewalk in front of her house. Too embarrassing for everybody.

So I waited for her by the park bench (yes, *that* park bench).

"Maybe I'll make a joke about it," I thought. When I saw her coming, I stepped behind the tree, where I could still keep an eye on her. Nobody else was near—good thing there.

I couldn't believe what happened next. As she neared the tree, she actually slowed down. She stared at the tree and brushed the hair from her cheek. She had no idea I was watching her.

I finally spoke, in the weirdest deep voice I could muster.

"Have you ever read a book about a talking tree?" I growled.

"Ooooh!" she shouted, dropping her books and stepping back so fast she almost fell off the curb.

I quietly walked around the tree. Without looking at her, I began picking up her books from the sidewalk. Faye was breathing hard and trying to recover. I could feel her look burning the back of my neck.

"I hope you're not mad at me," I growled.

Faye began laughing, quietly at first, then louder and louder, shaking her head.

"I'm so mad I don't know whether to kick you or . . ."

"Hey, don't say it!"

"I wasn't going to," she said.

"But you thought it."

"How could I not?" she said, still laughing. "We're here by the tree."

"We need to give this tree a name," I said.

"Whatever we name it," Faye said, "it can't begin with a K."

"Why not? We can call it Kicking Tree."

More head-shaking laughter. "I like it, Bobby. I like it a lot," she said. "In fact, that can be your Indian name. From now on, I'll call you Bobby Kickingtree. And that's final."

"Hey! Don't I at least get a naming ceremony?"

"Of course, Bobby. But that will have to come later, after you've killed the growling monster."

"Hoke, I don't mind waiting," I said. We looked at each other and smiled. I handed her the stack of books. I wanted to say, "You really do love books," but decided against it. Instead I asked, "Mind if I walk you to school?"

"Not at all," she said. We walked almost a block in silence. Happy silence.

I broke it. "You know I'm Choctaw? We used to have a naming ceremony."

"I didn't mean to make fun of you, Bobby."

"I know that, Faye. But someday I'll tell you a story about a Choctaw boy with no name."

"I'd love to hear it," she said.

"You know we are avoiding something. It has to do with what you told me at the Kicking Tree," I said.

"I know, Bobby. That's why I waited for you, hoping to see you before school. Any ideas?"

"Yeah. We keep an eye out for each other and don't make a big deal about our feelings. And we keep our eyes and ears wide open. The answer will be there, right in front of us; we just have to see it."

"Wow. You sound like a true believer in good beats evil."

"And forgiveness helps it along," I said. "That's part of the Choctaw way, Faye. Stay on the good road."

"You're about to make me cry again," Faye said. She stopped walking, and I watched as she slowly lifted her hand. She reached behind her head and touched the place where Heather had grabbed her hair. "Not easy to forgive or forget," she whispered.

I took her hand in mine. "I'm here for you, Faye. It's gonna be alright. Now, we better get to school. Growling Monster hates it when we're late."

She gave me a good-natured slap on the shoulder and whooped a loud laugh. "You'd make a joke if your house was burning down."

"No, that happened to my great-great-granddad," I said. "But later on that. Let's get a move on."

"Wait! I forgot something."

"Faye, we have five minutes to get to school. I'm not waiting."

She ignored me, of course. She gave me her books and scrambled through her purse for a pen and paper. "We'll make it," she said, as she wrote in a fury.

"Growling Monster is angry," I growled.

"Here," she said, slapping a note in my palm. "It's my class schedule. I don't want you to walk me to class. Not even. But just so you know when I'll be where."

"Got it," I said. "But for now, Faye, you're on your own." I gave her hand a quick squeeze and took off running.

I've never hurried so much between classes in my life. Trips to my locker, dashing to Faye's hallway, making sure she was still alive, then lowering my head like a mad bull and barely making it to my own class before the bell rang.

All day long.

Man, if I wasn't in shape before school, I sure was by the time basketball practice rolled around.

Oh yeah. That. My first day of basketball practice since I drove Johnny's car into Lake Thunderbird.

As any ballplayer knows, the real action takes place off the court. I had only started one game, which we won, and the team was 4–3. Four wins and three losses. I knew Coach Robison expected me to start, but I was the young Choctaw kid. Maybe everybody didn't go along with the coach, since he's Choctaw too.

I dressed in a hurry, keeping to myself. Then I saw him. Lloyd Blanton, a senior who now had my starting role. Shooting guard.

He was a good shooter, but the three-point line was a little out of his range. And since he moved only to his right, the turnovers piled up. Once his defender caught on, double-teams on that side of the court became a real problem.

So why was he a starter?

He hustled like his life depended on every play. I had to respect that. As he opened his locker and pulled out his shorts and sneakers, I eased up beside him.

"Hey, Lloyd," I said. "I'm coming back today, you know."

"That's what I heard."

That's all he said. *That's what I heard.*

He didn't look at me. He just kept putting on his playing gear.

"I hope we both get some playing time," I said. "You've earned your spot. You hustle your butt off. And, you're the upperclassman."

Lloyd laughed and turned to face me. "Hey, Bobby. We need to win some games. I just wanna be on the court if you ever miss a shot. Your Cherokee buddy can't get every rebound."

"Thank you," I said, holding out my open hand. He looked at it, gave me a senior smile, and we shook hands like old friends.

You never know when a small moment will mean so much in your life. I will never forget Lloyd's handshake.

CHAPTER 5

Shattered Glass on the Court

"Boys, get on the court. Now!" Coach Robison stuck his head out the door of his office and yelled so loud we knew something was big-time wrong. *"Now!"*

Those of us still in the dressing room hurried past the office and to the court. Mr. Blanton, Lloyd's dad, stood behind Coach Robison, and from the look on his face, he was not happy.

"I guess he's heard you're coming back today," Johnny said, joining me on the far end of the court.

We grabbed balls from the rolling rack and started shooting. I dribbled a few times away from the goal, and Lloyd snuck up behind me.

He slapped the ball in mid-dribble and sent it rolling crosscourt.

"Yeah, welcome back, Bobby!" shouted another senior. "We got your number!"

But the good-natured fun of teammates didn't last long. We heard a loud crashing sound and froze. Shattered glass flew from the coach's office and onto the court.

Mr. Blanton still held the chair he used to break the window. He turned and faced Coach Robison. "You might think everybody's happy with a wild Indian coaching our kids, but you're wrong!" he shouted, waving the chair back and forth in front of our coach.

We stood and stared, the whole team, unable to move, not knowing what to do. Coach Robison kept his hands at his sides. He never lifted them to protect his face.

He knows Mr. Blanton will never hit him.

But Lloyd thought differently. He pushed his teammates aside and ran into the office. His dad didn't see him, and Lloyd was able to wrestle the chair from him and toss it out the door.

"Dad, what are you doing?" he said. "Coach Robison is the first coach to give me a chance. I've been on the starting team now, my senior year. That's what you said you always dreamed about."

"You don't know him, Lloyd," his dad said. "He's about to bench you for that Indian boy— Indian like him," he added, pointing to Coach.

"Tell him, Coach," Lloyd pleaded. "Tell him I still get to play."

"Get to play is not good enough! You are a starter, now and for the rest of the season. And when you want to shoot, you take your shot, son. I am on your side here."

"No you're not, Dad. You're not fighting for me. You're doing this for yourself, so you can brag to your drinking buddies at the bar. That's what this is all about."

"You little smart-mouth!" Mr. Blanton said, raising his fist to Lloyd's face. "If we weren't on school property, I'd knock your teeth out."

Coach Robison had watched from the sidelines long enough. Seeing Lloyd threatened, he stepped between the two. He took Mr. Blanton's fist in his own and lowered it.

"I will make you a promise," he said, looking Mr. Blanton square in the eyes. "But you must promise me something in return."

Mr. Blanton squinted his eyes and sneered at Coach. "Your promises don't mean nothing to me." He spit on Coach Robison's desk, grabbed Lloyd, and turned to go.

"If you leave now, I'm calling the cops," Coach Robison said. "Your choice."

For the first time in the past half hour, Mr. Blanton listened. The word "cops" has that effect on some people.

"Okay," he said. "Let's hear it." He still held Lloyd by the wrist.

"For the remainder of his senior season, Lloyd will start every home basketball game. Maybe not on road games—that will be my choice."

"What's gonna hold you to that promise?"

"My word. I give you my word."

"And what do you want from me?" Mr. Blanton asked.

"I want you to promise you will not lay a hand on your son, for any reason, for the remainder of the basketball season."

"You can't tell me how to raise my son."

"And you can't tell me how to coach."

"We have a brave coach," said Jimmy, another senior. His voice was so quiet only we ballplayers heard him. Johnny nudged me in the ribs and whispered, "Yeah."

What seemed like an hour took maybe twenty seconds. Coach Robison stuck his hand out and Mr. Blanton took it.

"Promise?" Coach asked.

"Promise," Blanton replied, and they shook hands, looking each other in the eyes. Mr. Blanton gave Lloyd a fatherly swat on the backside, saying, "Now get to work, son."

Lloyd joined us on the court, his head hung in shame. We surrounded him, offering good words and shoulder hugs. But the scene in Coach's office wasn't over yet. Mr. Blanton was almost to the outside door when he turned and walked back to the office.

"Act Two of the craziest play I've ever seen," Johnny said.

"Coach," Blanton said as he entered the office.

"Yes?"

"You know I run a construction crew? How about I send two men out tomorrow morning to replace your window and repair any damages. No cost to you or the school. What do you say?"

"I say that'll be fine. I'll have the boys sweep up the glass before we start practice."

Mr. Blanton nodded and left the gym. Seeing the look on Lloyd's face, I'm guessing he knew where his dad was headed—to the nearest bar.

"Bobby," Coach Robison shouted as he exited his office. "Why don't you and Lloyd show how you can work together? There are brooms in the janitor's closet. We'll shoot and warm up at the other end of the gym while you two clean up the glass."

"Mind if I help too?" Johnny said. "I'm as much a part of the problem as Bobby."

"No, you are not, Johnny. Everybody, gather around for a minute. Have a seat," Coach said.

We surrounded him, sitting on the floor.

"Let's get one thing straight here before we continue. No one is a problem because of who their mother and father and grandparents happen to be. Is that clear? Does everyone understand what I'm saying?"

"Yes, sir," we all said.

"We are a team, and we are about to start winning some basketball games *as* a team. Are you ready to win?"

"YES, SIR!" everyone shouted.

"Good. So let's get started. We've wasted enough time already. Let's line up for lay-up drills, then baseline jumpers, then straightaway jumpers. No defense, but no slacking off. Drive hard and get ready to play. We're going full-court today, man-to-man press."

Lloyd and I agreed, without saying a word, to forget everything his dad had said and done. We did smile a few times and shake our heads as we swept the floor. We tossed the glass shards into the Dumpster outside and soon took our places in line for the shooting drills.

I felt great, taking a few dribbles and soaring to the basket, banking lay-ups first on the right, then the left side of the basket.

The baseline drill involved running around a screen, catching a quick pass, and taking a jumper—ten to fifteen feet from the basket. I missed my first shot, but no others. I relaxed and hit seven in a row, backing up a step or two after every shot, till my last shot hit nothing but net, sweet and true.

CHAPTER 6

Nice to Meet You, Left Hand

The full-court scrimmage was way harder than I expected. Coach Robison mixed the starters and the subs, so this was no "first team versus second team." Lloyd and I were guarding each other, but we'd already proven we could get along.

After all, we did share the same problem. We both had dads with drinking problems.

First time down the court, with Lloyd handling the ball, he dribbled hard to his right. I let him go, all the way to the baseline. He picked the ball up and looked for a teammate to throw it to.

I glanced at Johnny, but he'd already seen what I was doing. He left his man open under the basket and joined me in a trap.

Johnny waved his long arms so fast, up, down, and sideways, while I made a swipe at the ball. It bounced out of bounds, off Lloyd's knee.

Coach Robison blew his whistle and pointed in the other direction, giving us the ball.

"Two on one's not fair," Lloyd said, as we ran downcourt.

The next two times downcourt, I guarded Lloyd straight up and let him drive to his right. Tommy set a screen for him at the free-throw line. I saw the screen and knew I could fight over it and keep him from getting a clean shot. But something inside told me: *You can make this right. Give it a chance.*

I decided to do something I had never done before, and would never do in a game. I bumped into Tommy on purpose. I let myself get caught up in the screen so Lloyd could let his jump shot fly.

Make it, please. Let it go in. I didn't want to jinx it, so I didn't watch.

"Yeah!" Tommy shouted, so I knew Lloyd had scored. His teammates gave him fist bumps as they fell back on defense.

"Wow, Johnny," I said quietly, "they're acting like that never happened before."

"I can't remember the last time," Johnny said.

"For real?"

"Real as can be. And who do you think you're fooling, getting caught by that skinny-boy screen?"

"Guess you caught me, big Johnny. Now, ready for some pocket change?"

I lobbed the ball high to Johnny, who had worked his way around the post defense. He could have banked it in for a lay-up, easy. But *nooooo*, Johnny had to get fancy.

He caught the ball with one hand, a few inches from the basket. Then he fired it back at me. I stood all alone in the corner, my favorite spot.

I caught the ball, stepped into my jumper, and followed through like I'd been practicing for a decade or more. How sweet the feeling of nailing a jumper!

WHAT? I missed!

But Cherokee Johnny was there, as always, to mop it up. Once again, instead of banking it for two, he fired the ball back at me.

The ball sailed over my head and out of bounds.

"Hey, Johnny," Tommy shouted, "careful not to scalp your friend!"

They laughed at us, even my newest friend Lloyd. He looked at me and shrugged his shoulders. I tapped my chest with my fist to let him know we were cool.

After ten minutes of hard scrimmaging, Coach Robison blew his whistle. "Hoke, boys," he said. "Divide up into two groups, opposite ends of the court for free throws. Two at a time, and let's see who makes the most. The loser runs laps while the winner gets a water break."

Johnny and I knew it was a smart move to separate, hoping it wouldn't always be us against them. I made nine out of ten, but our team lost anyway. So Lloyd and Johnny headed to the water fountains, while me and my team circled the court.

"Bobby," Coach said, "time for you to take a break."

"You'll get no argument from me," I said, leaning over and clutching my knees. I breathed hard and felt the burning in my chest.

"Have a seat and watch how your replacement does," he said, with a serious look.

He is already planning something. Smart man.

Coach blew his whistle loud and walked to center court. "I need the starting five! Get in your positions on offense. And second string, pick up a man to guard."

Lloyd looked at me, as if he expected me to jump up and take his place in the starting five. I stayed seated, and he hurried to the point-guard spot at the top of the key. Coach Robison threw him the basketball.

"Now, Lloyd, when I blow the whistle, I want you to drive hard to your right."

Lloyd nodded.

"Johnny, you're on the free-throw line with your back to the basket. When Lloyd starts his drive to the right, I want you to spin to your left and run toward the baseline. And Johnny, this is all important. You set a screen for Tommy, just outside of the key. Got it?"

"Yes, sir," Johnny said.

"Good. Tommy, you fake hard to the baseline, then cut back around Johnny's screen. You lose your man and get a wide-open jumper at the free-throw line. Sound good?"

"I like it, Coach," Tommy said.

"Now, here's the real magic. It's all up to you, Lloyd. You can drive better to your right than any player I've ever coached. And as you've learned, there's a good side and a bad side to always driving to your right."

"My man overplays me, fouling everything up," Lloyd said.

"Hoke, son, but stay with me," Coach Robison said. "We're about to turn a weakness into a strength, and your man will never know what hit him."

He had our attention now. I couldn't stay on the bleachers. I had to hear this close up. Coach Robison smiled and kept us waiting.

"You boys will never know how much I enjoy coaching you," he said. "You're my best team ever. We just need to win a few games, that's all."

"How about if we win the rest of our games, Coach?"

"Yeah, I heard that."

"Let's do it."

"Nothing but wins."

The entire team picked up the feeling, and Coach let the team spirit grow. We all looked each other in the eyes. *Magic moment.*

"You ready, Lloyd?" Coach asked.

"Yes, sir."

"Hoke, take the ball and start your drive. Greg, stay with him, guard him close, and overplay him to the right. Don't make it easy. Understood?"

"Yes, sir."

"Good!" Coach said. "Lloyd, when I blow my whistle, stop hard. Everybody else stay where you are for now." Then he shouted, "Go!"

Lloyd took two quick dribbles to his right, and Coach Robison blew his whistle and clapped his hands.

"Now stop!"

Lloyd, with his back to his defender, pounded his left foot to the court and came to a quick halt.

"Don't move," said Coach Robison. "Stay right where you are."

Coach Robison was enjoying this more than any practice of the year. We could see it on his face. "Any ideas?" he asked.

Nobody answered.

"Anybody see a problem with the play?"

"Yes, Coach," I said. "If Lloyd is driving so hard to his right, how can he get the ball to Tommy at the free-throw line?"

"Yes!" Coach shouted. "I know this will work. And to answer your question, Bobby, he can't. There's no way he can get the ball to Tommy. Not yet, he can't. And Bobby, that's where you come in."

I stepped back and my mouth dropped open. "Uh," I muttered.

"Lloyd, give me the ball." Lloyd tossed the ball to Coach. "Watch closely, kids."

Coach Robison took two hard dribbles to his right, just as Lloyd had done. He stopped hard by pounding his left foot to the court. Just as Lloyd had done.

Then he pivoted back, on his left leg, spinning around to the free-throw line. All in one motion—with his left hand—he fired a pass across the court and into the far bleachers.

"Where were you, Tommy?" he asked.

"Coach, you said to stay where we were," Tommy said.

"I know. I was joking. But if you *had* been on the free-throw line, you would have an open shot with nobody even looking at you."

"Whoa!" we said in unison. "Wow!"

"Have you figured this out yet, Lloyd? Bobby?" Coach Robison asked.

We both nodded and smiled, looking at each other.

"That's right, boys. You have a lot of practice before I can turn either one of you on the court with this play. But the sooner the better. And Lloyd, there's another option to the play."

"What, Coach?"

"When the defense figures it out, you spin around and fake the pass. You'll be wide open for that fifteen-foot jumper you never miss."

I couldn't believe it. Coach Robison had come up with a play that used Lloyd's skills, played to his strength, *and* brought us together.

"I arrive at school an hour before classes start," Coach said. "If you two want to get here early and practice your spin move, the gym is open. But you better have all your homework done. Understood?"

We fist-bumped our reply. Oh yeah. This was gonna be fun.

"And Lloyd?"

"Yes, Coach?"

"You better introduce yourself to your left hand."

"I got it, Coach."

CHAPTER 7

Lloyd Plants a Kiss

All's well that ends well, right?

Hoke, but nothing ever really ends.

After practice we showered, dressed, and left the gym. I hung around waiting for Johnny. Before the accident, he'd always given me a ride home.

"You got enough gas to give me a ride?" I asked, holding the gym door open for him.

"Yeah, for sure," he said. "As long as you behave and do what I say."

"That'll be the day," I riffed.

"Where'd you get that one?"

I had to laugh before I answered him. "It's an old song Dad used to play when he drove around town drunk all the time. And man, if you said a word while this song was playing, he would cuss and threaten to beat you to a pulp! That's what he'd always say."

I will beat you to a pulp!

"What does that even mean?" Johnny asked.

"I don't know. Maybe you can ask him."

"Hey, stop for a minute," Johnny said, grabbing me by the arm.

"What's up?"

He walked around the corner of the building and motioned with a head tilt for me to follow him. "Be calm. No drunken rages, hoke?"

"Hoke, Johnny, just tell me what this is all about."

He pointed to the parking lot, where Lloyd was holding his car door open for his girlfriend. She had to be his girlfriend. He leaned over and gave her a quick kiss before closing the door.

"Oh no," I said, shaking my head.

"It's far worse than *oh no*," said Johnny. "Way worse."

"Something is not right here. Of all the girls in the world, Lloyd is dating *her*."

"Looks that way."

"And why is she staying after school, anyway?" I asked.

"Maybe she's been to the library."

"You trying to be funny?"

"Nothing else to do," Johnny said.

We stood in the shadows of the school and watched—while Lloyd and Heather drove away.

"I don't know how to tell Faye. You know she's been bullying Faye, yanking her hair, making fun of her all day in the hall. Between classes. At lunch. Faye can't even eat in the cafeteria anymore."

"Everybody in school knows, Bobby," Johnny said.

"Then why doesn't anyone do something about it?"

We walked to his car without saying what we knew was the truth. *Faye is not one of us.* That's what they're saying. You can do anything you want to her because *she's not one of us.*

"That means Heather will be at all the basketball games," Johnny said, once we were in the car.

"I was hoping Faye could come to the games. Man, this is bad, Johnny. Once Heather sees her, it's all over. She'll get her little crowd of girlfriends going. They'll make up a chant. You know they will. The same kinda thing they do for other teams."

"Any ideas?" Johnny asked, as we pulled onto the street.

I thought about the day, how cool practice had been. How smart Coach Robison was—to come up with an idea to bring the team together.

"Turn around, Johnny," I said.

"Hey, I'm not letting you get yourself in trouble. What are you thinking?"

"I'm about to break Rule Number One for every high school student."

"And what's that?"

"I am about to seek the advice of an adult."

Johnny screeched on the brakes and pulled to the curb.

"You're gonna do what!"

"I'm gonna ask Coach Robison for his help."

"Have you thought this out?"

"Yeah, Johnny, for almost a minute. Now turn this junk heap around and take me back to school. I want to catch him before he leaves."

Coach Robison's Chevy was still parked in the teachers-only spot by the gym. "He'll give me a ride home, Johnny. Thanks," I said, hopping out of the car.

"Will you call and let me know what's going on?"

"I promise, Johnny. No worries."

I stood on the sidewalk and waited for Johnny to drive away. Part of me wanted to jump back in the car. Heather, Faye, Lloyd, my coach, my dad, my struggling mom—where does it all end?

I had to laugh at myself. Jumping back in the car would be the same as climbing into my backyard hole in the ground. "Yeah," I whispered to myself. "That's where I want to be."

"What are you doing here, Bobby?"

I jumped a foot in the air in surprise. "Oh, Coach. Sorry. I didn't know you were there."

"Yes, son. I work here. And you?"

I laughed and hung my head. When I finally looked up at him, he had already figured out something was wrong.

"Is it your dad, Bobby?"

"No, Coach, Dad is fine."

"Then what is it?"

"I've got a problem with Lloyd."

"What did he do?"

"No, Coach. I said that wrong. It's not Lloyd. He's fine. It's his girlfriend."

"Who's his girlfriend?"

"Heather. Do you know her?"

"Oh yes. I've heard about her and your friend Faye. Kinda makes you wish you were still in that hole of yours, doesn't it?"

"You're a mind reader, Coach."

"You gotta be if you're gonna coach in high school, Bobby. So, you want my help coming up with a plan. Am I right?"

I nodded and stuck my hands in my pockets.

"First thing, let's get you home. We can talk on the way."

As he pulled out of the parking lot, Coach Robison took a deep breath and gave me a look that said "I'm with you on this, Bobby."

"Maybe this is a good thing, Bobby."

"How's that?"

"You answer that, Bobby. Think about it."

"At least Lloyd is not my enemy anymore. Maybe he can talk to Heather."

"Bobby, Lloyd never was your enemy. Don't ever forget that. He's trying to survive with a dad who drinks too much. You should know what that's about."

"Coach," I said, and a light turned on in my mind, bright and clear. "That's why you put me and Lloyd together, why we're working together, isn't it? So I can help him with his dad."

"That's one reason, Bobby. And another reason? So I can get along with his dad. He's even tougher than your dad."

Ten minutes later he turned into our driveway. He put his car in parking gear and was about to turn the engine off when he froze. He looked at me. My jaw dropped.

"Wow," I said. "I never thought I'd see that."

"Me either, Bobby."

My dad was on his knees, pulling weeds from the front flower bed. In the center of the bed stood a bright-red rosebush, newly planted.

Dad stood up, slapped the dirt from his hands, and pointed to the roses. He had the biggest smile on his face.

CHAPTER 8

More than Broken Windows

"Coach, do you notice any change in Dad since he stopped drinking?" I asked.

"No, why do you ask?"

"Oh, I dunno. He seems a little less serious than before."

"Maybe he has changed. A little," Coach said.

I laughed and looked at Coach. "You know, there was a time when I was afraid to even think anything bad about him. I'd be afraid he'd see it on my face and knock a few teeth out."

"Bobby," Coach said, "he never knocked your teeth out."

"How do you know?"

"I asked him one time, when he was talking about whipping you till you cried like a baby."

"Can we talk about something else?" I said.

"Good idea, Bobby," he said, turning off the ignition. "But you brought it up."

"It's hard to get some things out of your mind."

"We'll work on that."

"At least he is tough enough to face what he did."

"Hey, Buck!" Coach shouted, stepping from the car and greeting my dad.

"Looks like you kept your star basketballer after practice," Dad said, slapping Coach's palm with a warm and manly handshake.

"Yeah," said Coach, "and we have a small problem."

I jerked my head around and stared hard at Coach. I couldn't believe he was bringing Dad into the Lloyd-Faye-Heather scene. Coach didn't look at me, but he must have felt *my* look.

He squeezed me on the shoulder as he spoke to Dad.

"Bobby, you're not giving your coach a hard time, are you?" Dad asked.

Man, have times changed. In the old days, just the thought of me causing trouble would have sent me flying into the flower bed—the flower bed now beaming with Dad's bright-red roses.

I had to smile.

Will you please move on and let New Dad claim his place in the world?

"No, Dad, I'm not the problem, I promise you." I looked to Coach.

"You need a break, Buck," Coach said. "Can we sit on the patio and have a few beers?"

"Not funny," said Dad.

"Root beers," said Coach. "And yes—funny. Bobby, will you play bartender?"

"Man, what am I gonna do with you?" Dad asked, shaking his head and leading us through the garage to the patio.

I filled three glasses halfway with ice and to the top with root beer, and joined my two man buds.

"Fixing the broken window is not solving the problem," Dad said, and I knew which road the conversation was taking. "Don't you have to report what he did? Aren't you required to do that?"

"Yes. I already filled out the paperwork. I'll be meeting tomorrow morning with the principal. He will have to report to the district office. But I feel certain, as long as he repairs the window and causes no more problems, that the district will not file charges."

File charges! I hadn't thought of that. But it made sense. Lloyd's dad had destroyed school property and threatened a school employee. In front of students.

This was more serious than I had imagined. And I thought my dad was the craziest rampaging idiot I'd ever seen. But even Dad never destroyed school property.

Then another thought crept into my mind.

If he smashed a window with a chair and waved the chair in Coach Robison's face, what has he done to Lloyd?

Coach and Dad must have read my mind. They both took a sip of root beer and looked to me.

"You think he'll keep his promise?" I asked.

"Oh, I fully expect to see a repair crew early tomorrow morning," Coach said.

"That's not the promise I'm talking about, Coach."

"You mean his promise not to hit Lloyd."

Dad leaned back and his eyes grew wide. He was hearing this for the first time. "Whoa," he muttered under his breath. "It's getting deep." Then his eyes went to me. He covered his mouth with his fist and I knew what he was thinking.

"Hey, Dad, we're cool now," I said. An important lesson of the "No Name" story is forgiveness, and when it comes to Dad, I'm all about forgiveness.

He nodded and patted my hand.

"I also can't ignore his threat to his son, promise or no promise," Coach said.

"I think I know where this is going," said Dad.

"I know you're a mind reader, Buck, but you don't have a clue why I'm here."

"Hoke, let's see," Dad said. "How about tickets to a Thunder game? How's that for a big-time wager?"

"You're on," said Coach. "Hoke, what am I asking you to do?"

This was so cool. It was like I was invisible. No! Better than that! Both Coach and Dad were giving me my first glimpse into the world of beer-drinking men, even if it was root beer!

"You're asking me to head to the bar again, as soon as possible," Dad said.

"No way!" I shouted. When jaws dropped and they stared at me, I added, "Sorry, but I just couldn't stay quiet and listen to that ridiculous idea."

"Well, Bobby, my little basketball star," Coach said, "your dad just won free tickets to a Thunder game, for your entire family. And my wife and I will tag along too."

"Dad, you can't start drinking again!"

"I'm not going to the bar to drink, son," Dad said, as he and Coach bellowed out the belly laugh of the week. When they finally settled down enough to speak, it was Coach who explained the plan.

"Bobby, I'm asking—or I was about to ask—your dad to find Lloyd's dad and have a talk with him."

"And the easiest place to find him is at the bar. And I know he and I share one thing," Dad said.

Coach and I waited without saying a word.

"We are both angry drunks," Dad said. "The worst kind. My biggest worry is that he'll take his anger out on Lloyd. As I know, promises mean little when the fire takes over."

"What if he keeps the promise and takes his anger out on Lloyd's mother?" I asked.

The silence told me they were thinking the same thing.

CHAPTER 9

Under the Spell

"I have a few friends I can call," Dad said as we entered the house. "They can let me know when Blanton appears at the bar. They know when to keep a secret, so I'm not worrying about them saying anything to him."

"Buck," Coach Robison said, "you know how to talk to him. Go easy, but make sure he understands how close he came to being arrested."

"I hope I can talk some sense into him," said Dad, and I knew he was asking himself if this would have worked with him.

Coach shook Dad's hand, thanked him, and drove home.

For the next few days, Mr. Blanton must have done his drinking at home. Dad received no calls. And I was glad to get back to basketball.

Lloyd and I showed up at the gym an hour before school started every day. "What's up?" he said, greeting me on our first day of before-school practice. We both wore b-ball shorts and carried our school clothes rolled up in a bag.

"Let's do some dribble drills first," I said, "to get that left hand strong. I can use the work myself."

We both dribbled a hundred times—around the back, through the legs—all with our left hands only. I had forgotten how hard a behind-the-back dribble was with no right hand.

"Oh man," said Lloyd. He kicked the ball across court and dashed after it.

"Hey, Lloyd, just remember you're not the only guy who can't go to his left. This drill is helping us both, big time."

"I just hope I can do it," he said. "It's like dribbling with a shovel. How do you do it?"

"It's all about the muscles, Lloyd," I said. "You build up the muscles on your left arm, especially your left wrist, and it gets easier. You'll see."

When I kicked the ball, trying to dribble through my legs, Lloyd picked up his ball and gave me a suspicious look.

"You did that on purpose," he said. "I'm not buying it. You're better than me at this ball-handling stuff. I know it. So just don't act like you aren't."

I had to laugh. "Hoke, Lloyd, sorry. But I'm on your side, dude. You gotta know that."

"Let's take a break," he said. "How about some jumpers from the free-throw line?"

Lloyd started on the left side of the court and drove hard to his right, even with the free-throw line. He stopped on a dime, then jumped high and turned—in midair—to face the basket. He let fly with a high, arching shot that kissed the rim on the way down.

"Nice shot," I said. "That's why Coach added this play, Lloyd. You've got a sweet jumper from fifteen feet away, and this new play will get you open."

"Let's shoot twenty apiece and keep score," I said. And was I in for a surprise. I usually took my shots from the corners, or sometimes straightaway from the top of the circle. Fifteen feet, no problem—or so I thought.

What I did not consider was Lloyd's ability to dribble quick to his right and suddenly stop, then transfer all that energy into his jump. Me? I almost always faced the basket. I missed my first three shots.

"That's enough," said Lloyd. "One more miss on purpose and I'm outta here. Besides, classes start in twenty minutes."

"Hey, Lloyd, I'm not missing on purpose. I'm out of my league here. Gimme a break."

"Wait till I tell Coach about how you can't hit a wide-open jumper from the free-throw line," said Lloyd.

"You don't have to tell me anything. Nothing goes on in my gym without me knowing it," Coach Robison said, stepping out of his office.

"How long have you been there?" Lloyd asked.

"Since the beginning of the year, when I accepted the coaching job," he said. "And it seems like forty hours a day instead of sixty a week."

Lloyd and I picked up our basketballs and headed to the dressing room.

"Not yet," Coach said. "By my count you still have seven shots to go, and Lloyd has a three-to-nothing lead."

"Yeah, I'm on it," Lloyd said. He dribbled with his left hand to the starting spot, switched to his right, drove to the line, and sank another jump shot.

"Man, you're making it hard for me," I complained, then hit the next three in a row.

Lloyd beat me, eight to five, and I was happy for him. But, since basketball is a competitive sport, I was not entirely happy.

"Good job, boys." Coach said, "Now get dressed and hustle to class. If you're late the first day, we all get in trouble."

Lloyd and I made it to class with five minutes to spare. As we hurried from the gym, I was reminded of another complication. What happens when Heather decides to wait for Lloyd?

She already did wait for him after practice. What happens when she and Faye are both standing around outside the gym, before school, waiting for their boyfriends?

I guess I could call her my girlfriend. She kissed me. I kissed her. Doesn't that qualify?

I entered first-period English and tried not to stare at her.

There she was, my Mystery Lady Faye, sitting by the window and watching the December breeze blow leaves from the trees.

"Shut up," I told myself. "You are a basketball player, a varsity starter. You are not a poet, so cool it with all this romance stuff."

I plopped my books on the desk and took my seat.

"How did practice go?" Faye asked from two rows away.

Muffled laughter came from several classmates.

As I turned to face her and give her a wide-eyed cool-it look, I caught the scent of her perfume. I tilted my head and blinked a few times, helpless and confounded by Mystery Lady Faye.

"Did you hear the assignment?" Mrs. Porter asked.

"Uh, yes, ma'am. No, I'm sorry. I guess I wasn't paying attention."

The whole class laughed at this one. I ducked my head between my shoulders. "Sorry," I muttered.

"Jerry," she said to the student sitting next to me. "Let Bobby know what we're doing today so he can join us."

"Yes, ma'am," Jerry said.

Thus began my first day under the spell of Mystery Lady Faye.

CHAPTER 10

Coming Off the Bench

On day two of our early morning practice, Coach added a new drill.

"Bobby, I want you to stand on the free-throw line, waiting for the ball. And Lloyd, what's your job?"

"I'll drive hard to my right, then pivot back and fire a pass to Bobby, for him to take a shot," Lloyd said.

"You're right so far," said Coach. "Now, can you tell me what's so special about this play?"

Lloyd and I both had to smile. "I'll fire the pass with my newest friend," Lloyd said. "My left hand."

"Yeah," I said, and Lloyd and I did a little two-step fist bump.

Coach Robison blew his whistle and stepped off the court. I moved to the free-throw line and Lloyd began his dribble. Two dribbles and ten feet later, he stopped and pivoted, with his back to his invisible defender.

With his left hand only, he scooped up the ball and fired a pass in my direction. Hoke, so maybe he didn't fire a pass. Let's say he floated a pass in my direction. But it did arrive chest high, perfect for my shot.

"Good pass, Lloyd," Coach said. "You'll get there."

"Thanks, Coach, but I've got a long way to go."

"But you're on your way, son. And here's another drill to help you get there."

He pulled a roll of tape from his pocket and marked an X on the floor next to Lloyd. "Stand here, Lloyd, and take a few dribbles with your newest friend, then throw the pass. No pivots. Just dribble and pass."

"How many times, Coach?"

"Till your arm falls off, son. But don't worry, it'll grow back before this afternoon's practice."

"Can I have his old arm for a souvenir?" I asked.

"Sure thing, Bobby," Coach said. "You can nail it to your door." Then he blew his whistle and stepped to his office.

Something about Lloyd's left arm hanging from my backyard door reminded me of Dad's favorite Led Zeppelin song:

Good times, bad times

You know I've had my share

I said a quiet prayer in hopes that good times were ahead, for both of our families, Lloyd's and mine.

We practiced twice a day, and the week sped by with no big dramas. No smashed windows, no calls from the bar, no bad bullying.

Faye and I decided that Heather had a short attention span. She had moved on and was now picking on one of her own friends, a friend who had made an A on a math test.

"Hey, let's go get some burgers and fries after school," Heather said one day at lunch, dumping her tray in the trash can for everybody to see. "I'm not eating this junk food anymore. Who wants to go?"

Her friends waved their hands and giggled, just as Heather knew they would.

Suddenly she froze. She tilted her head and dropped her mouth wide open. With her hands on her hips, she announced, "No way are you coming with us, Miss Suzy—the school In-Tuh-Lect-Chew-ULL. You're too good for us."

I buried my head in my hands and hoped Faye hadn't heard her. But she did, and snuck up behind me.

"Don't worry, Bobby. I'm cool. At least she's after somebody else."

The week fast-tracked, and looming ahead was my first basketball game since the accident. I woke up Friday morning after a restless sleep. I hopped out of bed—and that's when it hit me.

Mom and Dad will be going to the game together. For the first time, both of my parents will sit together, drink Cokes together, and watch their only son play in a varsity basketball game.

"Be cool if I was on the starting five," I thought. Then another thought came to mind. I remembered Lloyd's dad smashing the window in Coach Robison's office.

No, no problem with my coming off the bench. Besides, Dad understands why, and so will Mom. They'll still be proud of me.

Proud.

Just like in the story "No Name." My dad will be proud of me. I hope Lloyd's dad is proud too.

Then I was hit with another thought. *What about Lloyd's dad? What will he do when I take Lloyd's place?*

As usual, I met Lloyd in the gym before school. "You ready to play?" I asked him.

"Ready as ever," he said. "I guess Coach wants to wait till next game to add the new play, since we haven't practiced it with Johnny and the full team yet."

"I guess so."

"Oh, and in case you were wondering, Mom and Dad *will* be at the game. A cop dropped by the house yesterday, while we were having supper. He and Dad talked for a few minutes. I don't know exactly what was said, but I'm sure it had something to do with the window."

"Can I ask you something, Lloyd?"

"Go ahead."

"Is your dad drinking a lot since that day?"

"He's cut back. Big time. And he's staying home. No trips to the bar. But we'll see how long that lasts. He's cut back before."

"How are things around the house?"

Lloyd looked at me without speaking.

"Sorry," I said. "I don't mean to be nosy. Just trying to help. You know I went through all this with my dad."

"Not easy, is it?" he asked, then shook his head fast, trying to make it all go away. "Things are a little tense between him and Mom. But better than the cussing and fighting when he's drinking heavy."

"And I thought I was the only one," I said.

"So did I," said Lloyd. "So did I."

Coach Robison joined us on the gym floor. "No hard workout today, boys," he said. "Let's take ten jump shots apiece from the line, then the same number of free throws. That'll be enough for today. I want you both well rested for tonight."

"Thanks, Coach," I said.

"Thanks for everything," Lloyd added.

If I'm lying, I'm dying. Ten out of ten jump shots for Lloyd, ten out of ten for me.

CHAPTER 11

Jump Shooter Lloyd

"I want you to think of this as the start of a new season," Coach Robison said, beginning his pregame speech in the locker room. "We've played hard and won a few, but lost too many. The real season starts now. We have the talent. Let's show that we have the desire to win and the determination to fight through mistakes, exhaustion, whatever stands in your way— *our* way.

"Think of every play on defense as a game changer. Fight through every screen, hit the boards for every rebound, go for every loose ball. And when you have the ball, play smart."

Coach cast his gaze across the locker room, looking every one of us in the eyes, letting us know his message was for the team. As he finished, he motioned for us to stand and join hands in a circle, bowing to the center.

"We are a team," he said quietly. "Let us always remember. We are a family. We are a team."

"Now, men—one, two, three—yes!"

Our family of fifteen, joined as one, sprinted to the court for our final warm-up drills before tip-off. Johnny and I wanted so badly to look to the stands and see where my parents sat, how close they might be to Lloyd's mom and dad.

I guess I wasn't as subtle as I hoped. Lloyd jumped in line behind me and whispered over my shoulder.

"Remember what Coach said? We are here to win a basketball game. You can't focus on the people in the bleachers. That's for later."

"Hey, Lloyd, you're not just a cool teammate," I said. "You're a mind reader, and boy did I need that."

"Hey guys, what about me?" Johnny asked.

"Oh yeah, sorry," I said. "I forget. Did your folks walk that Trail of Tears too? My dad says you rode in limousines."

"Not funny," Johnny said.

"Somebody's gonna have to fill me in on what this is all about," Lloyd said.

"Later, Lloyd," Johnny said. With a smile he added, "And you should talk to me first, not this uninformed Choctaw kid."

Through the entire conversation we were shooting lay-ups, grabbing rebounds, and running from one line to the next. No one else paid any attention to anything we said. Every small group had their own banter going on. Which was good.

Still family.

Go, Panthers, go!

Final huddle. I took a seat near Coach Robison, and the starters took to the court. Tip-off. Here we go!

Johnny lost the tip to a tall, skinny post man from the Rattlers. He tipped the ball to a quick guard, who waited for his teammates to settle into their offense.

"Hoke," I thought. "Looks like a slow-down offense, not a lot of fast breaking."

First play was a lob-in to the skinny post man, and Johnny was ready for the pass. He stepped in front, stole the pass, and hit Lloyd as he dashed down the court.

What happened next was hard to believe, but Coach Robison showed no surprise, almost like he had drawn the play up. Lloyd tossed the ball to Johnny at the free-throw line. Johnny turned to his defender like he was about to drive to the basket. Instead, he flipped the ball over his shoulder, back to Lloyd.

Nobody ever tossed the ball back to Lloyd. He never scored!

But things were different now. Lloyd took two quick dribbles to his left, then changed direction and drove hard to the free-throw line. He stopped on a dime, jumped high, turned to face the basket in midair, and shot the smoothest jumper I had ever seen in my young life. It floated in slow motion to the basket and rocked back and forth gently in the bottom of the net before falling to the floor.

No one expected this little guy to shoot, so no one even went for the rebound. The crowd went crazy. "Panthers, Panthers, go, go, go!"

I spotted Lloyd's mom and dad in the stands, and his dad was on his feet, shaking his fists to the ceiling.

Coach Robison leaned over and whispered to me. "You might have to wait awhile tonight, Bobby. Looks like your replacement has earned his spot." He let me shudder in shock for a moment.

"Only kidding, son. But you gotta admit, he's come a long way. With *your* help."

On the Rattlers' second trip downcourt, Jimmy blocked the skinny dude's shot, and the ball sailed out of bounds. That seemed to be their offense. Henry Lobstock, nicknamed Skinnyboy, was their leading scorer. We knew that.

And their offense centered around passes to the post. He was taller than most high school players and averaged over twenty a game. But our frontcourt was strong and quick, and tall enough. Jimmy, Johnny, and Darrell played tough defense around the basket. They blocked out and rebounded.

The problem in our losses was never our defense. Scoring—that was the problem. But not any longer. Coach Robison let me know he was counting on me for fifteen to twenty points per game.

And now we had a real scoring surprise. Lloyd the jump shooter! I was so happy, watching Lloyd come alive before our eyes. And if I ever had doubts about confidence being an important part of the game, Lloyd's play was proof.

Our time together, our mornings at the gym, had given Lloyd the confidence he needed.

We led by seven points at the start of the second quarter, 18–11. And how many points did I score in the first quarter of my first game back? Zero.

How many minutes did I play?

The same. Zero. Was I upset? Not for a minute.

"Bart, take a breather," Coach said. "Bobby, you and Lloyd will be our backcourt. Let's go with a full-court press and speed up the pace. When you get the ball, let's run. And Panthers," he said with a pause, making certain he had everyone's attention, "let's have some fun, hoke?"

He waved his arms, bringing us all together in the circle.

"Yes!" we shouted, lifting our arms to the rooftop.

CHAPTER 12

Cops in the Stands

Before play began, Johnny sidled up behind me. "You hoke?"

"I'm fine," I said. "Ready to play, but I'm way cool with sitting out the first quarter. And so, I'm sure, is Lloyd's dad."

"How about yours?"

"My first basket will be for him."

Johnny surprised us all and outjumped Lobstock, tipping me the basketball. I took two dribbles and passed the ball to Lloyd.

"NOW!" shouted Coach Robison, and we both knew what that meant.

Lloyd drove hard to his right, stopped quick, and pivoted around, with his back to the defender. I ran to the free-throw line.

"You can do it, Lloyd," I said to myself. "Fire that pass!"

And fire it he did, with his strong left hand. I caught the ball and popped a jump shot from fifteen feet.

"Nice dime," Jimmy said, high-fiving Lloyd on his way downcourt. But Johnny stayed behind, waving his long arms at the Rattler guard taking the ball out of bounds.

They were not ready for a full-court press.

The inbounds pass sailed high downcourt, and Jimmy outran Lobstock for the steal. A quick pass to Johnny for a lay-up. We were now up 22–11. The cheerleaders tossed each other around and in the air, leading the chant "Panthers, Panthers, go, go, go! Poor little Rattlers, no, no, no!" as our fans rocked back and forth to the rhythm.

That's when all Hades broke loose. (Out of respect for Mom, both Dad and I stopped saying "hell.")

A fight broke out in the stands. Ten rows up, people were grabbing two girls and pulling them apart. With everybody standing and trying to get a look at the commotion, it was impossible for me to see.

I did see one girl swinging her fists. The referees blew their whistles to begin play, but all eyes were glued to the fight in the stands. This had never happened at a high school game.

A hush fell over the gym as two campus policemen pushed and shoved their way through the crowd. They took a screaming girl by the arms and waved onlookers away.

"Take *her* and leave me alone!" she shouted, pointing over her shoulder. "Get your hands off me! She started it! Arrest *her*!"

On and on she went.

I looked at Lloyd. He was slumped to the floor, his head buried in his hands. Our biggest game of the year and Heather was being dragged out of the gym by campus police.

A local newspaper reporter, here to cover the game, was snapping pictures as they exited the gym. The refs blew their whistles again, once the court was cleared and ready for play.

"Focus!" shouted Coach Robison. "Lloyd, are you hoke?"

"Yes, Coach, I'll be fine."

We all gave him a shoulder slap, and Jimmy said, "We got your back, Lloyd. Stay cool."

I took one more look at the stands and wished I hadn't. Lloyd's mom and dad seemed to be arguing. Easy to guess why. Something about Heather.

Please don't let Lloyd see.

Prayer answered. Lloyd tossed me the ball, and the game began. Again. The Rattlers were already in their tight zone defense.

"Keep up the pace," Coach shouted, waving his arms and urging us to hurry. Lloyd threw a pass to Johnny, posting up on the free-throw line. Johnny faked a pass to me in the corner, then bounced the ball to Jimmy under the basket for a lay-up.

We had them where we wanted them now, no doubt about it.

Guard the shooters or guard the post? Pick your poison, as Dad would say.

The cheerleaders danced across the gym, waving their pom-poms and doing their best to get the crowd into the game. But they'd lost their bling. Anybody could see that. And during the next time-out, called by the Rattler coach to stop the bleeding we were giving them, I noticed that our troop of eight cheerleaders was now reduced to six.

"I guess Heather still has a few friends," I thought. "Following her to jail. Or wherever she's headed."

Johnny must have read my mind. "Man," he said, "we could score a hundred, and nobody's gonna even remember the game tomorrow. Except the brawl."

Oh yeah. The score. Thirty-one to fifteen, Panthers with a solid lead.

"Nice going, men," Coach said as we gathered around him. "Good hustle, way to move the ball. No standing around. You know the rules."

We all nodded and struggled to catch our breath.

"Bart," Coach said, "give Lloyd a break. Bobby will take over at point guard." He tapped a senior post player on the shoulder and turned to Johnny.

"Johnny, you've earned a break too. Nice dime."

We all had to smile at that one.

Nice dime?

Coach Robison was talking the talk!

I knew why. He was following that old Choctaw creed. Find laughter in the midst of tragedy. It helps you to survive. He would do anything to get our minds off what we had just witnessed.

But for me, the worst was yet to come.

CHAPTER 13

Building the Bridge

Without even thinking, I gave a quick glance to the stands, to Mom and Dad. Dad sat with his elbows on his knees and his head buried in his hands. Even from that distance, I swear I could see the veins in his neck, swollen and red. Mom sat by his side, hugging Faye close to her. Faye was wiping her eyes, so she had to be crying.

"Bobby," said Bart, tossing me the inbounds pass. Too late. It bounced off my forehead and out of bounds.

As I sprinted downcourt to play defense, I saw Coach walking to the end of the bench. I knew exactly why.

Looking for my replacement.

"Coach," I said as I passed him by, "give me one more chance. Please. One more?"

Coach turned to me with a big smile on his face.

"One more, Bobby," he said, holding up one finger.

Hoke, so even I had to laugh now. I knew I would never hear the last of it from Johnny. We could be eighty years old and treating our grandkids to ice cream, and Johnny would tell them all about the time "your grandpa dribbled the ball with his head! Ask him to do it again."

I made it up, hopefully, on the next play. As my man dribbled to the top of the circle, I fake-lunged at the ball. He did a cool crossover dribble and switched hands to his left, then turned around and slowly backed up. Closer and closer to the basket.

He looked over his shoulder and gave a small nod of the head.

"He's signaling the post man," I thought. "He's about to lob it into the post."

Some call it luck, but if you don't take chances, the luck never happens. I remember hearing Clyde Drexler, a former star of the Houston Rockets, say that once, talking about Russell Westbrook. So I took the chance. And I was lucky. I timed my jump just as he picked up his dribble and threw an over-the-head pass. I swatted the pass away, grabbed it as it bounced behind him, and streaked to the basket.

That was Chance Number One, and it worked.

Chance Number Two was even riskier. No one stood between a wide-open lay-up and me. But instead of taking the two points, I stopped at the three-point line.

"Take it, Bobby," Jimmy shouted. As I leapt into the shot, my mind did a time tumble, back to the first day I met Jimmy, Bart, and Darrell, at the park near my house. That was the day Jimmy busted Johnny's lip, elbowing him in the mouth.

"I know you can play dirty," Johnny had said, with his lip bleeding all over his shirt. "I want to know if you can play basketball."

And that was how we earned the respect of our future teammates.

I remembered my first shot that afternoon. Bart was guarding me when I took a long shot from the corner. It ripped the nets clean.

Something about the memory of that summer game at the park made me relax. I even smiled, and Coach later asked me what I was thinking.

But right now, my three-pointer hit nothing but net, and the gym erupted.

Panthers, Panthers, go, go, go!

We now led 34–15, and at the first chance, Coach called a time-out. "Everybody gather around," he said. While we huddled around him, he drew a play on his clipboard. Johnny, Lloyd, and I looked at each other, and it was hard to contain our excitement.

Coach had drawn up the play we'd talked about but never practiced. Lloyd drives hard to his right, then spins and fires a pass—with his left hand—to a teammate who's wide open on the free-throw line.

"Johnny, go back in. You'll be setting the screen on the baseline for Darrell's man. Darrell, you bump your man off and run to the free-throw line."

"Lloyd, remember what to do?"

"Yes, sir, Coach, "Lloyd said. "I pivot around and hit Darrell with a pass." As if he read our minds, Lloyd lifted his left hand and gave Darrell a high five.

The referees blew their whistles for play to resume.

"Go get 'em, guys," I shouted, and took a seat next to Coach.

Jimmy threw the ball inbounds, at the far end of the court. The Rattlers' defense was already in place. Bart dribbled across midcourt and tossed the ball to Lloyd at the top of the key. Lloyd faked a pass to Johnny at the free-throw line.

"Now we see how much he has improved in the past week," I said quietly. Coach heard me and patted my knee. We both wanted so badly for this to work.

Lloyd drove to his strength, as expected. He dribbled hard to his right and his defender overplayed him. But to the surprise of everybody, including Lloyd's dad, he stopped suddenly and pivoted, turning his back to his defender. He threw the pass with his left hand, just as we had practiced every morning for a week.

Johnny had already run to the baseline, setting the screen on Darrell's man.

The ball arrived at the same time Darrell did, fifteen feet from the basket. Darrell caught the perfectly thrown pass—chest high—and arched a high jumper into the net.

"Panthers, Panthers, go, go, go!"

In the eyes of casual fans, it was just another field goal, extending our lead. But our serious fans, those who knew our team, were flat-out stunned. There's no other word for it. They were stunned!

I'd never seen Coach jump out of his seat before, but he did, and he waved his fists at the gym roof. Anyone watching would have thought we had just won the state title. The feeling swept from one end of our bench to the other. We were celebrating.

And for Johnny and me—and Coach Robison too—we had something else to celebrate. In a quiet but important way, we were celebrating the building of a bridge. Coach Robison had built a bridge from start to finish.

He had shown the toughest parent of a Nahullo basketball player that he was fair. And that he could forgive. This tough-minded Nahullo had busted his window and threatened him with a metal folding chair, waving it in his face.

Yes, this was a night of revelations, and I had another one.

Oh man. There's a lot more going on between Coach Robison and Lloyd's dad than I thought. It's like what happened with my dad. Why didn't I see that?

Dad and I felt closer than ever after my accident. What happened tonight, that simple play we'd all seen, was a breakthrough moment. Lloyd's dad and Coach were on the same side. And for the first time, Lloyd's dad knew it. No denying it.

I glanced to the stands, and Lloyd's mom and dad were both on their feet. But while everyone around them cheered and clapped, his parents stood at attention, more of a quiet honoring of their son.

"Maybe this is what games are really all about," I thought.

CHAPTER 14

Whimpering Dad

As soon as I had that thought, I had another. We still had Heather to deal with. And as happy as Lloyd was about tonight's game, he had to be worried.

To start the second half, Coach let the first teamers rest. That included me, since the Panthers now had six men as our starting five. I sat next to Lloyd. I knew Cherokee Johnny would understand. Besides, he was busy making friends with Darrell and Jimmy, his frontcourt teammates.

"You have any idea how scared I was when Coach drew up our play?" Lloyd asked me.

"Man, if you were scared, you sure didn't show it."

"I faked it good, huh?"

"Real good, Lloyd. I was sure glad Darrell made the shot."

"Yeah, that would have changed things," Lloyd said, "if he threw up an air ball."

"Oh, I dunno. Johnny would have swatted the ball to you, and you could have scored."

"Right," Lloyd said. "I coulda thrown up a three-pointer with my left hand."

We looked at each other and laughed like the friends we were becoming. I didn't want to spoil the mood, but I also wanted Lloyd to know I cared about him on and off the court. As the game drew to a close, I noticed he kept looking to the stands. I leaned over and whispered, so only he could hear.

"She won't be back tonight, Lloyd," I said.

He jerked his head around in surprise. Then he took a deep breath and tried to relax. "Is it that obvious?" he asked.

"No, not at all. But I know how I felt when my dad showed up drunk at the game," I said. "Remember?"

"Yeah. Man, I felt so bad for you. We all did."

"Same for you, Lloyd. You got nothing but friends on this team."

Lloyd hung his head and didn't say anything for the longest time. When he finally spoke, his voice changed. He looked at me with a smile and slapped me on the shoulder.

"Let's drop it for now," he said. "We have a victory to celebrate. Hoke?"

"You bet, Lloyd," I said. "We have quite a few victories to celebrate. Did you see how proud your folks were? They stood up to honor you, Lloyd!"

"You serious?"

"Oh yeah. Everybody around them was cheering and clapping. But they kept hugging each other and staring at you. I'm not kidding."

"Alright," Lloyd said. "Let's keep quiet about that too. Do you mind?"

"You got it, Lloyd," I said, laughing my head off.

With the game over and all the dressing room towel-popping antics complete, we stepped to the lobby of the gym. More parents than usual greeted us. Everyone got to play tonight, we won, and almost everyone had scored.

So parents welcomed their boys—to the embarrassment of many.

"We want to take you out for pizza!" said Harold's mom. Harold was a junior and almost never played.

"Dad?" Harold said, pleading with his old man to get him out of this. He had his own car and plans for the night. After all, it was a Friday. No school tomorrow.

"Oh, don't worry, son," his mom said. "You can sleep in late tomorrow. And you have all weekend to do your homework."

"Yeah, Mom," said Harold. "That's what I was worrying about. Dad?"

His dad just shrugged his shoulders and rolled his eyes. "Nothing I can do, kid," his face said.

And that's how it often is, when we "children" do something to make our parents proud. All the celebrating is with *their* friends, not ours, and on *their* turf. But I wasn't complaining. I knew Mom and Dad would be waiting for me in the parking lot.

We hadn't planned it. I just knew it. And Dad would be at the wheel of his pickup truck, making some joke about the last time he waited for me in the high school parking lot.

"Hey, Bobby," he said as I approached his truck. "Remember the last time I waited for you after a game? You decided you'd rather go swimming than spend time with your dad!"

Wow. That was pushing the line. Even for Dad.

Hoke, so I did take a dive, if you wanna call it that.

That night when I left the game, I saw Dad, who had just been thrown out of the gym for showing up drunk. He was standing by the roadside, near Lake Thunderbird. He was waving his arms at me, with the coolest father-friendly look ever. Like he was asking for me to forgive him.

So I did. I let go of the steering wheel, and the car I was driving smashed through the fence and dove into the lake.

"Yeah, Dad. I remember." I smiled and jumped in the truck beside Mom. "Don't have long. The team is meeting for pizza, and you can't come. But let's go out for something quick. That hoke?"

"Guess so, Bobby," said Dad. "Hon," he said to Mom, "can you find me some Kleenex? I'm about to cry. Dearest little Bobby is too proud to hang out with his sweet mother and lovingly tender old man. Whimper, whimper."

I reached over Mom and patted Dad on the shoulder.

"Aww, shucks, Dad," I said. "Forget my friends and Coach Robison and the pizza. Let's you and I go have a few beers. Mom can tag along if she wants."

"Bobby!" Mom said with a stern look. "That's going a little far, don't you think?"

"Yeah, Bobby," agreed Dad. "Whimper, whimper. Where's my Kleenex?"

I was having the best time ever with the parents, but it only lasted four minutes tops. Two blocks from the parking lot we passed by a patrol car with its lights flashing. It had pulled over a car full of teenage girls. They sat quietly in the car, too terrified to move.

But leaning against the car, hollering and waving her arms, was Heather.

CHAPTER 15

Panthers Celebrate

Dad circled the patrol cars and drove slowly by, three blocks to the nearest hamburger stand.

"Cokes and ice cream?" he asked, pulling into the lot.

"Sure," I said. Mom had not spoken since the incident.

"It'll be hoke, Mom," I said. "There's not a lot we can do."

"I know, Bobby," Mom said. "I'm just thinking about her poor mother."

"And I'm hoping Lloyd's dad drives the other way," Dad said. "Don't want him involved in this."

"Why can't a basketball game ever be just a basketball game?" I asked. "What a way to celebrate."

"Because life doesn't work that way, son. Just ask your mom."

Dad walked around the truck as I hopped out. He waited for me to move aside, then reached for Mom's hand to help her step from his truck. He then hurried to the hamburger stand to hold the door open for Mom.

I smiled and shook my head, realizing that Dad was performing for me, demonstrating the gentleman he had become. It was all in good fun.

But the look on Mom's face was one of sheer joy. On one level this was all a big joke. But on another level, I was watching the rebirth of the man I knew as my father.

"Yakoke," I whispered, looking to the sky. "Thank you."

I ordered a root beer float, and Dad and Mom each had a soda and a scoop of ice cream. Dad went for chocolate and Mom strawberry. We soon took our seats and dove in.

"Ummm hmmm," said Dad.

"You played so well, Bobby," said Mom, wiping ice cream from her lips and reaching for my hand.

Suddenly a siren sounded and a cop car sped by, weaving in and out of Main Street weekend traffic.

"I know where's he's headed," Dad said. "I saw Blanton speed by as I pulled into the parking lot. He's got himself in trouble."

He stood up and motioned for us to follow. Mom hesitated.

"Buck," she said, "there's nothing you can do. Not now."

"You don't understand, hon," Dad said. "This might involve Blanton, Lloyd's dad. I have to make sure he keeps his head. He might be drinking, and I've got to stop him."

Mom grabbed Dad by the wrist, and he turned to face her.

"Please, Buck," she said. "You can go to the police station. Later. But you cannot get involved in a street brawl. Not now."

I could not believe what was happening. In the old days—not that long ago—Dad would have flung her arm aside and pushed her. Hard. He would have cursed at her and left us both.

This was a new trial. A new challenge for Dad. *Please, Dad. Please.*

Dad took two steps back and plopped on the bench at our table. He buried his head in his hands. "Oh my," he muttered. "Of course you're right. I could end up in jail along with him."

He looked up, and tears filled his eyes. "How in Hades did you ever stay with me?"

"You know the answer to that," Mom said, and kissed him on the forehead.

"I can step outside," I said.

Mom and Dad turned to me—as if they were seeing me for the first time. As if they just now remembered I was here.

"Uhh, sorry," I said. "I don't want to be in the way."

Dad laughed first. Mom soon joined him, and Dad spread his arms wide and pulled us all together. My mind went back to that miracle night in the hospital, when Dad promised he would never drink again.

On one condition. If I came back alive.

We must have been quite a sight—two parents hugging a teenager in a hamburger stand on a Friday night. Too weird for words. The manager tapped Dad on the shoulder.

"Excuse me, sir," he said. "Can I help you?"

"No thanks. We're doing fine," Dad said.

"Better than fine," added Mom.

We looked back and forth at each other, flipping our eyes from side to side—almost as if we were on the same page. After a nice round of laughter, we slurped and smacked and ice-creamed our way to three bellies full.

I had to fight a constant thought as I ate. This was a very strange night. I felt as if I had more in common with my parents—*my parents!*—than I did with my friends.

Hoke. That's not true. Johnny and Lloyd and Faye and I saw things from the same side of the mountain. We were close. But this much also was true. For the first time in my life, my mom and dad were not trying to drag me down into the pothole of their lives.

Nope. No more potholes. No more backyard holes. No more No Name.

We soon hopped in the car, and I reminded Dad to drop me off at the pizza place. "The team's waiting on me, I'm sure, Dad."

"Oh yeah, Bobby. They're all staring at the pizza on their plates. Nobody would even think of taking a bite till hero Bobby arrives."

"You got it, Dad," I said. Kinda fun in a way, jive talkin' with the old man.

Dad drove a little more carefully than usual, and I knew he was still thinking about the evening. Cops. Fights in the bleachers. Jail for some, school expulsion for others.

As he turned into the parking lot of the pizza kitchen, he said, "Bobby, wait just a minute. I want to visit some more with you and your mom. Not tonight. You need to celebrate with your Panther buds. But maybe we can have a family picnic tomorrow afternoon. That possible?"

Mom turned her head slowly, with wide eyes and a sly grin on her lips. "A family picnic?" she asked. "I like that idea. You're serious, right?"

"Sounds good to me too, Dad. But don't stay up past your bedtime."

"And just when is my bedtime?" Dad asked.

"That's up to Mom."

"And your mom is still trying to figure out how to raise two boys," Mom said.

"Grown-up boys," I said.

"Yeah," Dad said. "Well, why don't you get your grown-up hiney out of my truck and give your mom and me some grown-up time together?"

"Sure, Pops," I said, hopping out of the truck. I joined my teammates for pizza, finally, as Mr. and Mrs. Byington headed home.

"Hope you like pepperoni," Johnny said as I pulled up a chair.

"Hey, Bobby!"

"You been downtown, Bobby? Firing away!"

"No! Bobby's been practicing the head bounce!"

Happy times, happy greetings.

Everyone sat at a long table in a far corner of the restaurant. Since we'd won the game, a blowout, we had earned the right to be loud. Respectfully loud. Coach Robison, after all, sat at the head of the table.

At ten o'clock sharp, Coach stood up and announced, "Hoke, boys. We've got a noon run-through, to get ready for Monday's game. You can expect the south side Tulsa bunch to be a little tougher than tonight's opponent. Just a quick hour, noon to one. See you tomorrow, and nobody be late!"

"Coach, do we pick up our own tab?" I asked. "Uh, and I'm not joking. I got here late."

"The Panthers Booster Club is paying for tonight's pizza, boys. So let 'em know you appreciate it if your folks are members."

I climbed in Johnny's car for the short trip home.

"You see Faye after the game?" he asked.

"No, but something tells me I might have an underground date when I get home."

"Good thinking," Johnny said. "Give me a call and let me know how it goes."

"If I don't call tonight, I will in the morning."

"Need a ride to practice?"

"Yeah. Thanks, Johnny. And nice game. I'm still reeling about our new play. Lloyd oughta be feeling good about now."

Johnny said nothing. He waited for me to realize how foolish "Lloyd oughta be feeling good about now" sounded.

"Oh man," I said, after a moment of silence. "How quickly we forget. Did anything come up at the pizza place?"

"No, we all treated Lloyd like you said. Like he'd made the play of the game. Which I guess he did."

"How serious are he and Heather?"

"I'm sure he's on his way to her house now," Johnny said.

"I'm not so sure about that."

"Why? What's up?"

"Lloyd's dad might be in jail about now. Dad saw him speed by the hamburger place, where we were. And a few minutes later, a cop car drove by, lights flaring and sirens blaring."

"Wow. What else can go wrong this evening?" Johnny said. "This reminds me of a Shakespeare play."

"Which play?" I asked.

"How am I to know?" said Johnny. "But something from one of his tragedies has to fit."

"You are one crazy Cherokee, Johnny. And FOS."

"FOS? No way."

"Uh-huh. Way. Funny Only Sometimes. What did you think FOS meant?"

CHAPTER 16

Popcorn in the Hair

Johnny dropped me off at the house. The lights were still on in the living room, and Mom and Dad were watching the late-night news.

"Bobby," Dad said as I entered the house, "your mom and I decided to wait till morning before we call anybody about tonight. We're too tired to stay up late worrying about something we can't do anything about. Make sense?"

"Sure does, Dad. Makes a lot of sense. And just so you know, I'm still in the dark. Nobody talked about it at the pizza place. We celebrated the win, and even Lloyd faked it. He's the one I'm worried about."

"Me too, son," Mom said. "I hope he's strong enough to survive."

"He's got lots of help, at least from his basketball friends. And Coach Robison too."

"You have one smart man at the end of your bench, Bobby," said Dad.

"And two cool folks back home. You two are the best. Hoke, bedtime for Bobby. I've got practice from noon to one tomorrow."

"And after practice?" Dad asked.

"Picnic with my Choctaw elders. Achukma! Good!"

I was glad Mom and Dad chose not to get involved in whatever was going on with Heather and Lloyd's dad. I'm certain they were praying about it. It's not that they didn't care. They understood that real caring often comes *the morning after*.

That is often the case when alcohol is involved. You pick up the pieces the morning after.

But I couldn't help myself. I had to talk to Faye. I rang her number and she answered right away.

"Thank you so much for calling," she said. "Bobby, please believe me. I did nothing to get Heather in trouble."

"You don't have to convince me, Faye. I never thought that."

"Well, everybody else blames me," she said, and I could hear her fighting back the tears.

"Want to talk about it?"

"Bobby, I sat behind your mom and dad at the game. We talked some. We cheered when the Panthers scored. Everything was going so well."

"You want to tell me what happened?" I asked. "If you don't want to talk about it, I understand."

"Just give me a minute."

"You've got two minutes, and I'll call you right back. That hoke?"

"Sure," she said, and we hung up.

I stepped to the living room, where Mom was watching TV. Dad was nodding and falling asleep on the sofa.

"Dad?" I said, and he jerked awake.

"What? You hoke Bobby?"

"Everything's hoke," I said. "But I need a favor. Can I spend some time in my underground room? Faye needs to talk."

They looked at each other in silence.

"Yes," Dad said. Mom nodded her agreement.

I walked to the back patio and called Faye. In four minutes she slipped through the back gate and joined me. I held the door open and she climbed in.

"Popcorn?" she asked, pulling a bag from her pocket.

"Popcorn! Are you kidding?" I asked. When I was living in my underground room to hide from my dad, Faye had gotten me a microwave and rigged it up with a long extension cord plugged into an outlet on her patio, with leaves glued on the cord as camouflage. It was still there, just as she had set it up.

"Nope," she said. "I didn't get to enjoy my popcorn at the game. Heather knocked it out of my hands. She smashed it from the bottom up with her fist, so I had extra-buttered popcorn in my hair."

"I'm sorry, Faye." I said, feeling awful. "You're a quiet girl. You never get in anybody's face about anything. Why would Heather treat you this way?"

"Let's talk about that later," Faye said, with a determined smile—that's right, a smile—on her face. "Right now I need some popcorn."

She tossed the bag in the microwave and hit the button. Soon our underground hideaway was filled with the buttery, salty smell and the rat-a-tat sounds of popping corn.

"You sure you don't have a little Choctaw blood in you, Faye?"

"You mean because I'm being funny instead of crying?"

"That's what I mean."

"Well, if you want to know the truth," she said, puffing her cheeks and whooshing a huge breath of air, "I already cried my little eyes out. No more. Not tonight."

I let it go at that for a while. She took the bulging bag of popcorn from the microwave and ripped open the top, setting it between us.

"Count to ten real slow, and I'll be right back," I said, pushing the door aside and crawling out. I left the door open, since my underground home was no longer a secret.

When I returned with two chilled cans of grape soda, Faye was slowly counting to ten. She blew a "sev-un" into the night air. "You made it," she said.

We ate, drank, and did our best to be merry.

"Whenever you're ready to talk," I finally said. "But can I hold you first?" Faye nodded and pointed above us to the door. I tugged it over our heads, giving us the privacy she wanted.

Faye rolled my way and buried her face in my chest. I wrapped my arms around her. I could feel the pain building up, and I whispered, "I am here for you, Faye. That will never change."

For the first time since I met her, Faye completely let herself go, shaking and sobbing and clinging to me. We held each other tight and rocked sideways.

When the shaking stopped and the sobbing grew quiet, I ran my fingers softly over her cheeks. "We are together," I whispered. "And who could ask for more? You live next door— what are the chances?"

Faye made a funny, wide-eyed face as she glanced up at me, and I planted a kiss on her lips.

"What a crazy world we live in," she said. "So can I tell you what happened?"

"Please do," I said. "You know I would much rather talk about Heather than hold and kiss my sweet next-door neighbor."

"Good," she said, "then we're in agreement."

We laughed and kissed and held each other tight again. With her face still buried in my chest she stammered, "Are you ready to listen?"

"I'm ready, Faye. I need to know everything that happened if I'm gonna help Lloyd deal with this."

"That's the weirdest thing about the evening," Faye said. "You know I'm not into sports. I'm learning because of you, Bobby. But back in North Carolina, I only went to basketball games because my friends were playing. I never even tried to understand the game."

"It's pretty simple," I said. "Ball bounces off the rim or ball scores. That's when it falls through the round metal hoop. You know, the hoop attached to the glass square."

"I think I'll go get more popcorn," she said, in a voice thick with sarcasm.

"Sorry, Faye," I said. "I'll listen."

"Good. So when Lloyd scored and was playing so well, I started cheering for him, along with the cheerleaders and everybody else in the stands."

She paused and took a drink of her grape soda. I knew that trouble was coming.

"I didn't even see her," she said. "I was standing behind your mom and dad. I wanted to be close to them. You understand, right?"

"Sure. Close to neighbors, friends, my folks."

"I don't think Heather was sitting anywhere near us. I would have seen her, and trust me, I looked. I think she snuck up on me. And when I started cheering for Lloyd, that made her angry."

"What did she say?"

"She called me a name so bad I don't even want to say it. And when I ignored her, hoping she would go away, she yanked my hair from behind. She twisted me around and slammed her fist into my box of popcorn."

"Did my folks see that?" I asked.

"Not at first. They might have heard her shouting, but the whole gym was jumping up and down and hollering."

"Faye, they heard it. I know they did. Heather has that scratchy scream in her voice when she's mad. Everybody heard it."

"You're right, Bobby. I just don't want to admit it. Yes, everybody within a hundred feet heard what she called me. Then she started hollering about how I better leave her boyfriend alone. I better shut my mouth and get home to my books."

"Faye, what do you think this is really about?" I asked.

"It's bigger than Heather and Lloyd, Bobby. I think she can't take the changes going on all around her. She used to be the prettiest girl in school. But now pretty isn't everything. And Lloyd and his friends ruled."

"And now that we have a Choctaw basketball coach," I said.

"*And* Choctaw and Cherokee players," Faye added. "Things are changing."

"Smart matters," I said. "Pretty isn't everything. And you might not admit it, Faye, but you do have a fair share of pretty *and* smart."

"I never thought of myself as anything but a bookworm," Faye said. "And that didn't bother me. I do love books. I like to read and dive into a world that makes more sense than this nutty universe. And you wanna know what I like most about books?"

"I'd like to hear it," I said.

"In a good novel, good wins. That doesn't mean evil doesn't make a strong showing. But evil never wins. Not in my favorite books."

"You wanna know why I like life more than books?" I asked.

"Yes, I do," Faye answered. "I'd like to hear this."

"Hoke," I said. "In the world of books, evil might lose. Evil might even die. Or be killed. But seldom does evil have a chance to change. I want Heather to have that chance. I want Lloyd's dad to have that chance. My dad did, and look what happened."

"You want miracles," Faye said.

"Yes. I want miracles."

CHAPTER 17

Night in Jail

Saturday morning was usually a sleep-in-as-late-as-you-like day, but not today. The sun was peeping through my window curtains when I heard Mom moving around in the kitchen.

I looked out my bedroom window, and there sat Coach Robison and Dad on the patio, drinking coffee and talking quietly.

Man, I wish I could listen to that conversation. Guess I'll know soon enough. If Coach came over this early on a Saturday, it must involve Lloyd's dad.

"Or maybe it's just two old men relaxing over a nice morning coffee," I said to myself. *As if.*

I tossed on a Thunder T-shirt, jeans, and sneakers, and hurried through the kitchen.

"You're up early," Mom said.

"Looks like the whole neighborhood rose up early," I said.

She slid a glass of orange juice across the table and smiled.

"Thanks for the juice," I said on my way to the patio.

"Have a seat, Bobby," said Dad. "We were about to get you out of bed. No need for surprises."

I looked at Coach, but he waited for Dad to tell me the news.

"Lloyd's dad was pulled over for speeding last night. As we thought. He also swung a fist at a police officer. But he was so drunk he slipped and fell on his butt."

"Is he in jail?"

"He is for now," Coach Robison said. "Mrs. Blanton is trying to borrow enough money to get him out on bail. And the obvious question is, why doesn't she just get a bail bondsman? They're available 24/7."

"Which raises another question," Dad said.

"She doesn't want him out of jail," I said. "Sounds like Lloyd needs a friend. A friend who won't judge him for what his dad does."

A powerful silence hung in the air, and I realized what I had just said—in front of my own dad.

"Kinda like Cherokee Johnny and next-door neighbor Faye," Dad said.

"Sorry, Dad. I didn't mean anything by it. You know I love you, old man."

Dad smiled and gave me a light-fisted shoulder bump.

"And I, you, kiddo. But I understand what you're saying."

"Maybe you can give Lloyd a call?" asked Coach. "More than ever, he needs to be at practice today."

"Sure thing, Coach," I said, standing to leave.

"Not yet, you don't," Mom said. "Mind holding the door open for me?"

She carried a platter loaded with scrambled eggs and onions, with bacon bits and cheese decorating the top. Also on the platter were thick slices of just-juicy-enough bacon.

"And for my health-minded husband, I even made oatmeal and sliced bananas."

"Yum de dum," said Dad, rising to help carry toast and butter and jam and whatever else remained from the kitchen table.

"See what I've been missing all these years, Coach," Dad said.

"Yeah, and all for a sip of beer at the bar," added Coach.

"Hoke, fellows, mind if we talk about something else?" Mom asked.

We all laughed and joined hands for our prayer. Dad gave the offering. "Dear Lord, please bless this food and the lives of everyone at this table. Bless also those who need you the most, the mother, the son, and the man in need of higher understanding."

I didn't want to lift my head and open my eyes. I didn't want anyone to see the tears. Or see my face. I felt like I was rising from my deathbed, in the hospital once more, surrounded by Dad and Mom.

Maybe it was Dad's voice that brought back the memory. So strong. I don't know how, but I heard him say it again—as real as the night of the true miracle. "I can tell you this," Dad had said. "If he comes back to us, I will never touch another drink as long as I live. You have my word on that."

"Yakoke, Dad," I said, in real time now, lifting my face so all could see my feelings. "Thank you."

As we began eating, Coach Robison said, "I want to make sure Lloyd shows up for practice today. He can't be missing on his father's account. That would start a dangerous precedent."

I spooned salsa on my eggs and took a big bite. I was reaching for my orange juice when I realized everybody was staring at me, waiting for me to say something.

"Hoke," I said, after gulping down a swallow. "Why don't I call Lloyd and make sure everything's alright? Or as alright as things can be with your dad in jail."

"Why, Bobby, I think that's a wonderful idea," Dad said.

"Hoke, Dad," I said with a laugh, "that was a little over the top. I'm thinking that's what you two were hoping for."

"Better coming from you than me," Coach said.

"And to tell you the truth," I said, "I was gonna call him anyway."

"Good for you, Bobby," Mom said.

"Basketball for Lloyd is quite a bit different than it is for you," Coach said. The way he glanced around the table told me he wasn't sure if he should say this or not. So I waited.

"Lloyd will never play college ball. He hustles and gives it his all, but he doesn't have the skills needed to take it to the next level."

Where is this going?

"Whereas you, Bobby, are a bright student, a good learner on and off the court. And you have a natural ability to shoot that arching jump shot. You're a fine ball handler already."

Mom and Dad dropped their jaws and looked at me, then at Coach Robison.

"Are we talking scholarship here?" Dad asked.

Coach shrugged his shoulders, pursed his lips, and nodded a *yes* for all to see. "With a little work."

"Coach, maybe that's setting the bar a little high," I said. "I'm just a punk kid playing my first season!"

"Exactly my point," Coach replied. "You're playing your first season and already competing against seniors."

I was blown away.

"Excuse me, folks," I said, jumping up from the table. "I'm gonna make that phone call."

I hustled to my room, shut the door, and dialed Lloyd's number. After five rings it went to voicemail. I decided against leaving a message, but something told me to try again.

I waited a few minutes, and this time he answered the phone on the first ring.

"Hello?"

"Lloyd, this is Bobby. I just heard what happened last night. I'm so sorry, dude."

"That's hoke. Thanks for calling."

"You at home?" I asked.

"No, I'm at the county courthouse. It's not the first time Dad's been caught driving drunk."

"Oh man. My dad could have been pulled over a hundred times. He was very lucky," I said. "And Lloyd, I want to make sure you'll be at practice today. You were great last night. Let's keep it going. Hoke?"

"I don't have a way of getting there," Lloyd said.

"Johnny and I can pick you up. Can you be out front at ten thirty? Do it, Lloyd, please."

"Sure thing," Lloyd said. "You think Coach is gonna be mad about everything? Heather and now my dad?"

"I guarantee you, from the way he dealt with my dad, he'll be happy to see you. See you in a few," I said.

"Good news," I said as I returned to the breakfast bunch. "Johnny and I are picking Lloyd up at the county courthouse."

"The county courthouse?" Mom asked.

"He's not a first-time offender, I'm guessing," Dad said.

"Did Johnny agree?" asked Coach.

"Yikes!" I said. "Maybe I ought to give Johnny a call."

"Details, details," Dad said.

"Choctaw humor," I said. "Gotta love it, eh, Dad?"

"Gotta survive somehow," he said. "I hope you know how important your friendship is to Lloyd, son. And Coach, I still intend to have that conversation with Mr. Blanton. I'm hoping an old whiskey-drinking Indian can talk a Nahullo into putting his bottle away. Think that's possible?"

"Sure worth a try," Coach said. "Not gonna be easy, I'm afraid."

"Nothing ever is, where the bottle is concerned," Dad said. "Nothing ever is."

"Well, my friends, I best be going," Coach said, rising from the table. "I'm sure my wife has a few Saturday chores for this Choctaw before practice. See you all later."

"Chi pisa la chike," Dad said, giving a Choctaw farewell.

"Chi pisa la chike," Coach replied.

I hopped up to call Johnny, when Dad reminded me, "Don't forget, we still have that Saturday family picnic. Your mom and me and our Choctaw basketball star."

"Dad, is it alright if I tag along? I'd like to meet this guy!"

"Get outta here," Dad laughed.

Johnny was happy to help, as I knew he would be. With three bags of Mickey D's breakfast meals, we arrived at the courthouse at 10:25. Lloyd was waiting for us on the sidewalk.

"Hey guys," he said, jumping in the back seat.

"Anything exciting happening?" Johnny asked.

Nothing like cutting right to the chase. But Lloyd was cool with it.

"Nothing new," he said. "Mom waited for him to cool off and sober up. She's getting him out on bail now. And Dad's gonna blame her for paying too much for the bail money."

"Either way, there's no way to win," I said. "Sorry, Lloyd."

"Hey, I'm not. It's a way of life. I just hate that it happened now. We're gonna win some basketball games this year. And I'm getting to play for the first time ever."

"Yeah," said Johnny, "and tossing dimes and scoring buckets."

"From way downtown," I added.

Finally, we can talk some basketball.

Didn't happen.

Lloyd's phone rang, and I watched as he made a face and rolled his eyes before answering.

Not good.

"Can't talk now," he said. "I'll call you after practice."

We couldn't hear what was said, but from the scratchy hollering on the other end of the line, we knew who it was.

Sweet Heather.

My mind went to Faye, and I had to fight my own anger. *She has no idea how much pain and trouble she causes. And if she did, she wouldn't care.*

CHAPTER 18

Burgers for the Boys

Practice was short and fast, with three hours of workout crammed into one. "Ten up-and-downs!" Coach shouted, blowing his whistle.

We sprinted ten times from one end of the court to the other. Twice he blew his whistle and yelled, "No slowing down!" and "Your next opponent is running hard. You wanna win?"

When we finally gathered around the basket, breathing hard, he said, "Nice game last night. But you know that was the weakest team we'll face all year. Monday night will be a real game, and we'd better be ready."

"We'll be ready, Coach," Darrell said.

"We're with you, Coach," Jimmy said, and everyone joined in.

"Oh yeah!'

"We be there!"

"Bustin'!"

"In your face," said a sub.

"Hoke, boys," Coach Robison jumped in. "No more in-your-face talk. Understood? We leave that to the big talkers. We're basketball players. No rubbing it in."

"Sorry, Coach."

"Not a problem. Just don't want to hear that. Hoke, men, first team on the court!"

The best thing about Coach Robison? You knew exactly what to expect—the totally unexpected. And, once again, he banked it.

"Hoke, men, let's set up the offense. Second teamers, you're on defense. Come on! Let's move!"

My job was to guard Lloyd, our official starter at the point. I guarded him close, overplaying him to his right.

"Let's run the play I drew up last game. Any questions? Hoke, let's go," Coach said, tossing Lloyd the ball.

Lloyd gave his little head fake to the left, but I knew better than to go for that. Then he lowered into his dribble and drove to the right. I didn't make it easy, forcing him away from the basket. As he neared the sideline, he pivoted back to his right. He scooped up the ball with his left hand and fired a pass to Darrell at the free-throw line.

Nothing but net.

"Hoke, good job, Panthers," Coach said. He gave me a quick look before blowing the whistle. "That's the way to force him out, Bobby. Make him work for it."

"Thanks, Coach."

"Now, gather 'round. Only the offense." Coach talked low, so only the starting five could hear him. Then he clapped his hands and said, "Hoke, let's make it work."

He blew the whistle, and I saw they were running the same play. Lloyd drove hard and stopped on a dime, then spun around to pass the ball.

But this time I was ready. I didn't overplay him, didn't force him around me. No, I waited for him to pivot, then jumped back to intercept the pass.

I hate being outsmarted! I don't care if it is by a coach. But outsmarted I was. Lloyd only faked the pivot, and when I jumped to cover the pass, he drove right by me for a lay-up.

"Whoaaa!" shouted his teammates.

"Nice D," Johnny said to me.

"Don't bust your ankles," said Jimmy.

"Hey, you dropped something," Darrell added. "I think maybe it's your pride."

Everybody, Coach Robison included, had a big laugh at my expense. At first I was embarrassed. Coach knew what I would do. I didn't fool anybody, trying to steal the pass.

Then I saw the smile on Lloyd's face. He just drove through the defense for a score. "Nice fake, Lloyd," I told him. "You had me."

"Coach's idea," he said. "I just did what I was told."

"First time for everything," I joked.

"Let's try a new wrinkle," Coach said. "Bobby, you switch to offense, playing in the corner. When Lloyd drives, you take your man in, going for a rebound. Then cut behind him, back to the corner. That gives us some options. You with me, Lloyd?"

"Yes, sir, Coach. I can pass to Darrell at the free-throw line, hit Bobby in the corner, or drive to the basket."

"You've got it. Now, let's play!" He blew his whistle, and we went to work.

Ten minutes later, Coach let me take Lloyd's place at point guard. For the last half hour of practice, we worked on a full-court press. Coach blew his whistle, clapped his hands, and yelled orders—till we were all exhausted, fired up, and ready for the Monday night game.

"Let's call it quits for now, men. Get some rest," he finally said.

Everybody headed for the door, but Johnny waved at me to join him on the free-throw line. "I just want to shoot a few," he said. "Mind rebounding?"

"No prob, Johnny," I said, and joined him at a side basket. He was acting a little strange, so I knew he had another purpose.

He took two shoots and hit both. Then he said quietly, "What should we do with Lloyd? I know he'll get a ride with his old friends, but is it safe for him at home now? What do you think?"

"You're right, Johnny. No way he needs to be home. His dad will be busting mad. Let's go."

I hurried to the parking lot and caught Lloyd hanging out on the sidewalk. "Lloyd," I said, "let's go get some burgers. Johnny's treat. How about it?"

"Sure. Sounds good to me," Lloyd said. He looked relieved.

As we approached Johnny's car, I called out, "Hey, Johnny, me and Lloyd want to take you up on your offer. Free burgers and fries! Man, you Cherokees must be rich."

"Uh, yeah," Johnny said, narrowing his eyes and letting me know *you'll pay for this, dude.* "Sure thing. We have money for burgers. You got it."

Johnny drove as far away from Lloyd's house as possible, to an out-of-the-way burger barn. "Been awhile since I've been here," Lloyd said.

"Best burgers in town," I said. "And thick, old-time fries."

We soon chomped down on juicy, thick burgers. *So what happens next?* A moment later, the answer came to me.

"Lloyd, can we talk?"

He nodded, keeping his eyes on the table.

I scooped up a French fry dripping with ketchup before I spoke. "You've survived this before, I know. So have I. I had a hiding place when I knew Dad was drunk and mad."

"Sometimes Dad throws things around the house," Lloyd said. "Sometimes he takes it out on whoever is around. Then he heads to the bar."

"You know he won't be driving, not after his arrest," I said.

Lloyd looked out the window and kept his thoughts to himself. "We've got a spare bedroom," Johnny said.

I knew that wasn't gonna happen.

"So what about tomorrow," Lloyd said. "And the next day and the next. I'm a senior. Five more months. I can handle it."

"Lloyd, we just want you to know you've got friends. Friends who care and don't judge you or your family. You have my phone number, and if you have any trouble—call me. Get out of the house if you have to. Take off running— just leave. *Then* call me. Not to report your dad or get him in any more trouble, hoke. Just to take care of yourself."

"You're serious?" Lloyd asked. "If I call you at midnight, you'll come get me?"

"Absolutely, Lloyd. That's what Johnny would have done for me. No gossip, no BS, with teammates or anybody. Just you knowing you're not by yourself. Hoke?"

"Best burgers in town," Lloyd said. "Best friends, too."

CHAPTER 19

What Hideout, Where?

"Hoke, guys," Lloyd said, taking a swig of his soda. "Let's say Dad has me by the throat, and I ask him to let me go for just half a minute. He does. So I pull out my cell phone and dial one of you. Let's say you, Johnny, since you've got the car? But you're too busy downloading a movie on your iPad, so you don't answer. What then?"

"Wow," I said, looking at Johnny.

"Wow back atcha," Johnny said, and we high-fived across the table. "Now we're getting somewhere!"

"What are you talking about?" Lloyd asked.

"Don't you see, Lloyd?" I said. "You're joking about your dad choking you? That means, Number One: It's never happened."

"And Number Two," Johnny added, "you're beginning to trust us, or you wouldn't be making that sick, and I mean *sick* joke. Am I right?"

"You guys are crazy," Lloyd said, biting into his burger and chewing with a smile.

"But just in case something does happen," I said quietly, "I have an extra room. One very few people know about."

Johnny gave me a strong gaze, and a slow smile crept across his face. I could tell what he was thinking. *You're gonna show him the room.*

"Is this still a joke?" Lloyd asked.

"Not even close. This room saved my life. I'm sure of it."

"Yeah, I heard about how your dad drove your mom away. And you ran away for the summer."

"I didn't run away. I was home. All summer long."

"Let me guess," said Lloyd. "You were living in the attic, and your dad didn't know. And you only came down when he was gone."

"That's closer to the truth than you think," I said. "Johnny, you ready for a ride?"

"We going to your house?" Johnny asked.

"Yeah, maybe it's time for some house-cleaning."

"Hoke," said Lloyd, "If you're going to do chores, drop me by the house first."

"But this housecleaning is for you, Lloyd. Nobody but you," Johnny said.

We soon pulled into the driveway, where Mom and Dad were loading the car with bags of food and an ice chest.

"Yikes! I forgot to tell you guys. I'm supposed to go on a family picnic this afternoon."

"A *what*?" Johnny and Lloyd shouted in unison.

"Yeah, and I promised. Dad wants to share something with me, so this is important."

"Want us to come back later?" Johnny asked.

"No," I said. I felt a cool authority. *Dad and Mom can handle this.* "Johnny, you take Lloyd to the backyard."

As they rounded the corner of the house, Dad set down the ice chest. "What's going on? Did you forget our picnic?"

"No, Dad. No way. I'm excited. But Lloyd might need a place to go, so . . ."

Dad held up his hand. "Wait one minute, son," he said.

"But Dad!"

"I said wait. Hear me out, Bobby. I don't know why you're taking Lloyd to the backyard. I don't want to know. Neither does your mother."

"Wow, Dad," I said. "I think I know where you're going with this."

"Good. Because if we know nothing about Lloyd and your backyard underground room, if the cops come looking for him, we can truthfully say we don't know where he is."

"Or might be," added Mom.

"'Cause I'm not lying to the cops, Bobby."

"Of course not, Dad. Uh, I'll see you in five minutes, hoke?"

Dad nodded, and I joined Johnny and Lloyd standing behind the giant red oak tree.

"Lloyd," Johnny was saying, "what you are about to see has to stay a secret. Lives depend on it. No one can know, not for any reason."

"I understand," said Lloyd. "But why are we standing around in the backyard?"

I knelt down and tapped on the door a few times.

"Whoaaa," Lloyd said, with a bug-eyed look of amazement on his face.

"Nobody's home" came a voice from under the door.

"Faye? Is that you?" I asked.

"Who wants to know?"

"Faye, what are you doing down there?"

"Hey guys," said Lloyd, "somebody better tell me what's going on. This is weird even for you two."

I pulled the door aside and Lloyd took a few steps back. "Wait a minute," he said. "Is this where you went when your old man lost his temper? You have a backyard hideaway?"

"You got it, Lloyd."

"I'm not believing this. Did you dig it yourself? And how did you keep it from your dad?"

"I dug it myself, and hiding from Dad was easy. As long as he had his beer, he didn't worry about me."

"Sounds more like my dad than yours," Lloyd said.

"That was my *old* dad. He's not the same dad now, not even close."

And I'm not the same son I was back then, either. No Name, done and gone.

While Lloyd and I were trading dad stories, Johnny climbed into my room and was talking quietly with Faye.

"Mind if we join you?" I asked.

"Four's a crowd," Johnny said, "but let's do it."

I slid down and turned to Lloyd. "Come on in. Join the party."

To make my point, Faye tossed a bag of popcorn in the microwave. "I filled the ice chest with grape soda," she said. "Hope that's hoke."

"Achukma," I said. "That's cool."

Soon—huddled close and seated—we grabbed handfuls of popcorn from the bag and washed it down with ice-cold grape soda.

"Faye, maybe you want to tell them what you told me," Johnny said.

Faye covered her face with her hands and shook her head.

"It's about Heather, isn't it?" Lloyd asked.

"She scares me," Faye said. "I'm sorry. I know she's your girlfriend, but she won't leave me alone."

"I'm really sorry. But you won't have to worry about her for a while. She got expelled after last night's game."

"Oh no," said Faye. "She'll blame me for it."

"I'll talk to her," Lloyd said.

"No! Please don't. That would only make it worse."

"Maybe not," said Lloyd. "I've got an idea."

Before he could share his thought, Dad gave a shout-out from the patio.

"Bobby, my boy," he said, "your mom thinks you don't like her chicken fingers! It's picnic time."

"Sorry, but I gotta go," I said, climbing out of the hole. "Stay here if you like. Just turn the lights out when you leave. And Lloyd, remember to keep the secret."

"No problem, Bobby. Thanks for the welcome."

CHAPTER 20

Schoolin' the Old Man

"Dad," I said as I climbed into the car, "can we talk basketball? All this bully-racist talk is making me want to climb in a hole."

"Son, you already did that."

"Oh yeah, I did. Did it work?"

"Better ask your mother."

"Wish I had a hole to crawl into on our wedding night," Mom said. She had a hint of a smile in her voice.

"Hey! That's not funny!" Dad said.

"Well, Buck, you didn't have to bring your drinking buddies along on our honeymoon."

"Hoke, sweetheart," Dad said. "You got a point there! I promise I'll never do it again."

And so the fun family talk went, till Dad pulled into the parking lot of the nearby park— the park with the basketball goal, filled with memories.

"What's up, Dad? We can't have our picnic here."

"That's why you're the kid," Dad said. "You do what your parents say."

"What?"

Dad didn't explain. He just popped open the trunk and handed me the small space heater. No electricity needed.

"It's a little chilly, so we thought this might come in handy," he said. "You get to pick the table, and your Mom and I will arrange the food."

"Don't forget your sneakers, Buck," Mom said.

"Sneakers? Dad doesn't wear sneakers."

"I do when I play basketball, Bobby. Are you ready to be schooled by your old man?"

So while Mom set the table with fruit salad, chips and cheese dip, chicken fingers, and sweet mustard—and that was only for appetizers— Dad sat on the bench and laced up his basketball shoes.

"Where's the ball?" I asked.

"Floorboard, passenger side," he said. "And don't be long. I'll do a few warm-up laps."

"Yakoke, Mom. Thanks a lot. You had to be in on this," I said as I returned and tossed the ball to Dad.

"I knew you'd like it, Bobby," Mom said, laughing as she spoke. "He's come a long way in a short time."

"Yeah, I do like it, Mom." I tiptoed to Mom, motioned for her to lean over so I could whisper, then spoke loud enough for Dad to hear.

"Maybe I should let him win."

"That won't be necessary, Bobby. Your dad has been practicing," he said, spinning the ball on his middle finger as he strolled to the court.

I was impressed, but I had to laugh. So did Mom. She sat courtside in a lawn chair, clutching her cup of coffee.

"One-on-one, Bobby?"

"Sure thing. Make it, take it. You go first."

Dad tossed me the ball, a make-sure-you're-ready tradition in one-on-one. He walked to the top of the key and I handed it to him, then I bent my knees in good defensive posture.

Dad knew I would try to steal the ball, so he backed to the basket, dribbling left, dribbling right. He stood a good six inches taller than me and had long arms.

But could he shoot?

He pivoted right, and I jumped up to slap the ball from his hand. Even before my feet left the ground, I felt guilty. My dad. My very own old man, doing his best to make up for lost time with his only son.

And here I was, about to steal the basketball from him!

Or so I thought. Dad was smarter than that. Dad was only faking. He outsmarted me. Once I left my feet, he pulled the ball down and ducked under me for a lay-up.

"Nice shot, Buck!" Mom shouted, clapping and shouting like a cheerleader.

I caught the ball as it dropped through the net, then turned and flipped it to Dad. "That was lucky," Dad said, covering his mouth to hide the laughter.

"Something tells me you *have* been practicing," I said. "Nice shot, Dad."

Though the final score was three games to one, in favor of me, Dad showed off skills I never knew he had. I stole the ball a few times as he dribbled, and he missed some close-in shots. But he did land two long shots, one from the corner and the other from straightaway.

"Wanna go again?" I asked, when my final shot dropped through the net. Dad was already breathing hard.

"No, son, but I will shoot some free throws with you."

"Five at a time, first man to ten?"

"Sounds hoke," Dad said.

Any thoughts I had that Dad would feel better if he won a game were flat out wrong. He wanted to see, firsthand, what his son could do. He had heard Coach Robison talk about a college basketball scholarship, and he needed some proof.

So I gave it my all. We played four games of "first man to ten," and of the forty free throws, I made thirty-eight. I couldn't believe it myself.

And Dad? Twenty-eight out of forty. Not bad for an old man!

Mom was no longer clapping and cheering. She just sat in her chair and beamed at her two favorite people. She knew, more than anyone, the miracle of this day.

"Let's take a break," Dad said as my final free throw rattled home. As we gobbled our snacks and sandwiches, I said very little. I knew our first family picnic in a decade had another purpose.

"You know, Bobby," Dad said, wiping the sweat from his brow, "you've done something I never even thought about doing."

"What's that, Dad?" I asked, having no idea where this was going.

He took a long, deep breath before answering, and I waited.

He rubbed the back of his neck with his hand, as he always did when saying something that needed to be said, unpleasant as it might be. Mom stared into her coffee cup.

"I'm a big boy, Dad. I can take it."

"It's not like that," he said. "It's nothing you did bad."

I waited.

"Son, you figured out a way to forgive your old man. Like I never could."

"What do you mean, Dad? I knew Gramps. He was a funny old Choctaw, always talking about the trickster Rabbit. Why would you need to forgive him?"

"Hoke, Bobby, you're right about Gramps. He was a fun old man. Let's shoot some more free throws." He picked up the ball and stood up to go.

I grabbed his wrist.

"Dad, wait! Please. I want to hear this. You never said much about Gramps, ever. And you always dropped me off at his and Mawmaw's house. You never stayed to visit. There was a reason, wasn't there?"

I pulled Dad back to his chair.

"Please, Dad."

He shrugged his shoulders and rubbed the back of his neck again. With a serious smile—that's right, a *serious* smile—he sat down and began.

"I had a preacher once, the man who married your mom and me. He always shook everybody's hand and said goodbye as we left church. He pulled me aside one Sunday, and I will never forget what he said.

"'Mr. Byington, you carry a lot of weight on your shoulders. Memory weight. If you want to lighten the load, you have to tell someone. Share the load with a friend. I'll be that friend if you let me.'

"That's what he said. But I was too young and stubborn. I thought about the load I carried, but I never considered talking about it. I am ready to talk now. Anybody want to listen?"

Mom and I gripped his hands and nodded.

CHAPTER 21

Good Times, Bad Times

"Tell Bobby how we met," Mom said.

"You mean . . ." asked Dad, the question hanging in the air.

"Yes, how we *really* met."

"Hoke," said Dad, with his head down and a sly sideways look at Mom. "I was still in high school, a junior. It was a Saturday morning, and I was strolling downtown. By the courthouse. I happened to be sitting on the sidewalk, and your mom sat down next to me."

"And I have loved you from that moment," Mom said. "But I think you should tell Bobby why you were sitting on the sidewalk in front of the courthouse."

"Waiting for you?" Dad offered.

Mom tilted her head and blinked her eyes so we could read her thoughts. *That's not gonna cut it.*

"Why were you downtown, Mom?" I asked.

"I was on my way to meet some friends for our Saturday morning shopping trip, seeing if any dresses might be on sale," she said.

I looked at Dad, waiting for his reply.

"Oh, of course! Why was *I* there? Well, I had just spent my very first night in the courthouse."

I didn't say a word. I didn't have to. I looked back and forth from Mom to Dad. I knew he was skirting around telling me something serious and important. But the glances and the subtle humor between them also told me this was a miracle moment, not a tragic one.

Dad took a deep breath, pushed his hair back, and gave me a look I will never forget. *Hoke, Bobby*, he seemed to say. *No more No Name works both ways. I hope you are ready for this.*

"I'll cut to the chase," Dad said. "And it *was* a chase, Bobby. The night before, I was out drinking with some buddies. It was after basketball season and we'd decided this Friday night was ours. No girls, no dates. This was our time. A case of our favorite beer and a trip on the party ship. Any way we wanted it.

"We drove out of town, circling around the foothills, not too far from Robbers Cave. Bobby, you probably don't remember, but when you were a kid, we used to take you to that old hamburger barn out on the highway. Best burgers in town."

I nodded and encouraged him to continue. No reason to tell him I'd taken Lloyd there last night. But it was pretty cool.

"We pulled into the burger joint and four angels dropped from the sky. Actually, it was a carful of sweet Panther high school girls, munching on burgers and fries.

"I parked next to 'em and we started the talk. Things were going hoke till they saw us swigging the beer. They rolled their windows up and drove away. Well, angels or not, this was no way to treat Panther basketball players! No way.

"So we drove after them. I must have been a bit more inebriated than I thought, Bobby. Know what 'inebriated' means?"

"Yes, Dad. It was on a vocabulary test last week."

"What?" Mom said. "A word that means 'drunk' was on your vocabulary test?"

"Only kidding," I said, motioning for Dad to keep talking.

"This is the hard part, son. Not because I'm ashamed. I have done so many things I'm ashamed of, and you two are still with me. No, it's hard because I don't remember much of anything after pulling away from the hamburger joint.

"It was Sammy Tom's car, but I was at the wheel. He asked me to drive, so he could get stinking drunk, as he put it. I think I out-drunked him.

"Nobody was hurt, but the car was totaled. Some fool planted a tree too close to the highway. I woke up in the back seat of a patrol car.

"Dad told the cops he wasn't about to get me out of jail in the middle of the night. Can't say I blame him. Besides, he'd been drinking whiskey since he got home from work that afternoon. Just like every other day. Excepting weekends, when he'd take his first swig right after breakfast."

Mom reached for my hand and held it tight. In the old days, she would have reached under the table. But we were all in this together now. No need to hide.

"Your grandma came and bailed me out the next morning, apparently without telling Dad what she was gonna do. But his friends at the courthouse called him. As I was walking down the courthouse steps, he comes speeding around the corner in his old pickup truck. He came to a screeching halt in front of the courthouse. Didn't even try to park. He left his engine running and his truck in the middle of the road."

"Oh, Buck," Mom said. "It feels so real, like this was yesterday."

"Same for me," Dad said. "But I gotta go on."

He looked at me before he spoke again. "Bobby, I am so sorry for everything I did to hurt you. This has to stop. No more in our family. Not ever."

I paused for just an instant. I knew he felt this way, but now he was actually *saying* it. Not ever. No more.

"I am with you, Dad. You know that."

"Yes, I do, Bobby. Yes, I do." He ran his hand through his hair and rubbed the back of his neck. Then he continued.

"My dad slammed his door shut and rounded the truck. Mom and I stopped. She eased in front of me, but he was having none of that. He grabbed her by the arm and yanked her aside. I stood maybe four steps above the sidewalk. Dad stared hard at me. 'You'll be sorry you ever did this to your mother,' he said.

"Then he balled up his fist, leaned back, and hit me in the jaw. Harder than I've ever been hit in my life—to this day."

"Dad," I said. "I know I should be quiet and listen. But I have to say something. You never hit me. I know you feel terrible about how you were. But you never balled up your fist and slugged me."

"Bobby, I did shake my fist at you."

"But you never hit me."

"I shoved you. I . . . I never hit you because I could never get this out of my mind. I kept seeing my father standing over me, watching as I rolled down the courthouse steps to the sidewalk."

"Bobby," Mom said, "you will never be this way. Your dad has changed, and you have forgiven him. And so have I."

"I never forgave my father," Dad said. "We never made peace."

"Dad, you know what the Choctaw elders say. The old ones never leave us."

"So you think I can still make my peace with him?"

I said nothing. I wanted Dad to answer for himself.

"Maybe when the days warm up, early spring, we can visit my dad's grave. You've been there once, Bobby. But you were too young to remember."

"I'd like to go, Dad. We can sing 'Shilombish Holitopa Ma' together. Your father would like that."

"'Amazing Grace' in Choctaw," Dad said. "Yes, I like that idea."

A sudden gust of wind blew my dad's cap off his head. He smiled and whispered, "I love you too, Dad."

Watching Mom and Dad at the picnic table, I thought of the past year. I have learned so much. I learned that booze and bullying starts at home. Dad was raised in a home filled with more hurt and pain than I ever knew.

And when he grew up, he had to take his anger out on somebody. But my dad was not like his dad, and something in him, some hidden seed of caring for others, was finally allowed to grow.

I have—at last—my family.

Lloyd needs me, and I will be there for him, for the rest of our lives. And while Lloyd's father stews with hatred, and Heather blames everyone else for her problems, I know I cannot let their dark feelings steal the light from my life.

My mind drifted to Faye. Mystery Lady Faye. She was still worried about Heather. But with her tormentor gone from school, things *had* to get better. Maybe not perfect, but better. And I'll be there for Faye, just like she's always been there for me.

With my next thought I had to smile, so big and childlike that Mom said, "I think you need to tell us what's going on."

"Oh, nothing," I said. "At least nothing I wanna share with Dad. He'd make fun of me," I whined.

"Anybody in their right mind would make fun of a silly little punk like you, kid," Dad said, doing his best to act like he meant it.

"Hoke, Mom. If he wants to tease me, let's remind him who's the real basketball-playing dude of the Byington household."

As soon as I said it, I wished I hadn't.

"Hey, Dad! You know I didn't mean it!"

"That's hoke, Bobby," Dad said, and it was his time to whine. "I know I'm a loser."

"You're the biggest winner I know, Dad," I said, reaching for his hand. He brushed it aside and fist-bumped me instead. Then Dad did something I had never seen him do.

Hoke, I guess this is a day full of things I've never seen Dad do!

He started drumming on the picnic table. Not Indian powwow drumming, but rock drumming, and right away I recognized the rhythm. Soon he began singing that Led Zeppelin song—the song that played when I crashed Johnny's car through the fence and almost drowned.

In the days of my youth
I was told what it means to be a man.
Now I've reached that age,

I've tried to do all those things the best I can.

No matter how I try, I find my way into the same old jam.

Good times, bad times,

You know I've had my share.

I had to tell him. If we ever *really* hoped to be close, he had to know about that night. He had to see it through my eyes.

"Dad," I said.

"Yes, Bobby."

"Can I tell you what goes through my mind when I hear that song?"

"I gave you that CD, didn't I?"

"Yes, Dad. And I was playing it when I drove Johnny's car into the lake."

"Oh, son!" he said, and I knew he was about to cry. "I am so sorry. I didn't mean to bring back that night."

"No, Dad! Please, listen to me."

He looked at Mom and shook his head. "I didn't know," he said.

"Dad, let me finish. Please. When I think about that night, I don't remember crashing through the fence. I don't remember the car sinking into the lake. What I see—and what I never want to forget—is you, Dad. You! Reaching out your arms to me and patting your fist to your chest. You! Letting me know you loved me. That is what I remember, Dad."

"And I always will, Bobby. I always will." He leaned over to me and hugged me tight, a warm father-and-son hug. I didn't look at Mom, but I knew she had to be crying too.

"Bobby," she said, "do you remember the song I taught you when you were a little one?"

"Nope," I muttered, and Dad laughed because I was still caught in his snuggle. I lifted my face from Dad's grip and curled my eyebrows in a question. So Mom began to sing.

This little light of mine,
And I joined in:
I'm gonna let it shine.
This little light of mine,
I'm gonna let it shine,
And not even trying to hide the tears streaming down his face, Dad chimed in on the final line.

Let it shine, let it shine, let it shine.

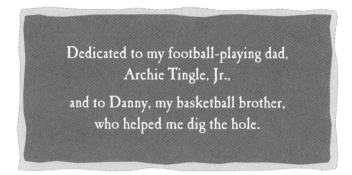

Dedicated to my football-playing dad,
Archie Tingle, Jr.,

and to Danny, my basketball brother,
who helped me dig the hole.

About the Author

Tim Tingle is an Oklahoma Choctaw and an award-winning author and storyteller. Every Labor Day, Tingle performs a Choctaw story before the Chief's State of the Nation Address, a gathering that attracts over ninety thousand tribal members and friends.

In June 2011, Tingle spoke at the Library of Congress and presented his first performance at the Kennedy Center in Washington, DC. From 2011 to the present, he has been a featured author and storyteller at Choctaw Days, a celebration at the Smithsonian's National Museum of the American Indian honoring the Oklahoma Choctaws.

Tingle's great-great-grandfather, John Carnes, walked the Trail of Tears in 1835. In 1992, Tim retraced the Trail to Choctaw homelands in Mississippi and began recording stories of tribal elders. His first book, *Walking the Choctaw Road*, was the outcome. His first children's book, *Crossing Bok Chitto*, garnered over twenty state and national awards and was an Editor's Choice in the *New York Times* Book Review. *Danny Blackgoat: Navajo Prisoner*, Tim's first PathFinders novel, was an American Indian Youth Literature Awards Honor Book in 2014.

7th GENERATION

PathFinders novels offer exciting contemporary and historical stories featuring Native teens and written by Native authors. For more information, visit: NativeVoicesBooks.com

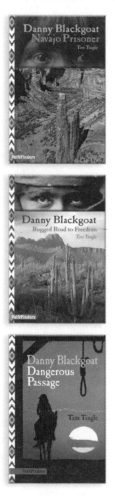

Danny Blackgoat: Navajo Prisoner

Tim Tingle

978-1-93905-303-9

$9.95 • 144 pages

Danny Blackgoat: Rugged Road to Freedom

Tim Tingle

978-1-93905-305-3

$9.95 • 176 pages

Danny Blackgoat: Dangerous Passage

Tim Tingle

978-1-939053-15-2

$9.95 • 168 pages